HER NAME IS SUMMER SKY

Le Anne Kemmish

First paperback edition February 2024
Book cover art by Le Anne Kemmish
ISBN: 979-8-218-40035-4 (paperback)

Published by Le Anne Kemmish
www.leannekemmish.com
Edited by Jennifer Lucas
Medicinal Plant References: Pacific Northwest Medicinal Plants by Scott Kloos

CHAPTER ONE

"You're nothing but a mutt" one of the boys taunted as he shoved Summer Sky. She bounced off someone behind her and caught herself before she fell. Another kicked her foot out from under her and she toppled onto the dusty path.

She stood and wiped the dirt from her skirt as best she could while waiting for the continuing onslaught of bullying. She searched for an adult for help. They must have all disappeared.

Children from the village surrounded her, pushing her one way, then again in a different direction like a ball tossed back and forth as if they were playing a game. But Summer Sky didn't like this game. The circle of laughing and taunting children shrunk. The bigger kids came closer. Her heartbeat quickened in cadence with her shallow breaths. One shoved and another tripped and down again she went. Back into the dirt. She thought about just staying there but that hadn't worked in the past. They'd kick her if she stayed down too long.

Summer Sky bit her lip, concentrating on holding back the tears. She had learned, from experience, the torment worsened if she cried. She should have gotten used to the abuse. It had become her life after her mother, Water Lily, had brought them to the village where she grew up after her father's accident.

"Yeah, your father was a pink bellied pig." An older boy kicked dirt into her face and spit at her, but she crawled her way through the legs of the others and gained her feet. She ran as fast as she could from the bullies. Once away, the tears appeared like a flood spilling from her eyes and tracing rivulets on her face through the grime. The dirt in her mouth ground gritty between

1

her clenched teeth.

"Summer Sky," one of the girls in the group called after her. She turned as a rock struck the corner of her brow. Blood gushed down her face and into her eye, mingling with the tears then dripped off her chin. She stumbled half blind. Summer Sky hoped her mother had duties elsewhere, but the flap of their home flew open as Water Lily rushed over.

Summer Sky saw the look on her mother's face as she ran toward her, angry, as they continued their taunts.

"Mutt, mutt, mutt" the children chanted in unison.

"Her name is Summer Sky," Water Lily hollered at the children who attacked her. Her mother wrapped protective arms around her and hurried into the tipi. Her mother would tend her outward and inward wounds, again.

Summer Sky had almost withstood their mean treatment. She'd almost gotten away if not for that rock.

If only I hadn't turned. It might have missed me.

But her experience had taught her the truth. If not that rock, another would have followed. If not this time, next time.

And she understood why they taunted and tormented her. Her differences. She would forever stand out while she lived among her mother's people. The small village they lived in, one of several villages along the Pend Oreille River in the Northeastern portion of the young State of Washington, which belonged to the Kalispell tribe.

She stood out, and she could do nothing about it. Her blue eyes would always set her apart. The glaring reminder of the difference between her and the other children in the village.

But where else would she fit in? Not the white people's town where they had lived on a farm with her father. Water Lily had said her father, Samuel Bishop, had many friends in the neighboring town and farms nearby. But her mother had only made a couple of friends in those eight years of marriage.

Her mother's gentle touch brought her back from the confusion of her life as she cleaned the painful wound. She could think of only one way of distracting herself from yet another assault. Talking about her father, above everything else, comforted her. Summer Sky suspected her mother had guessed her motive, but she never changed the subject.

"Mama?" Her mother stopped washing the dirt from her face.

"Tell me about Papa."

CHAPTER TWO

Water Lily gazed upon her daughter's smudged face wishing she could have given her a better life. She still grieved for Sam whom she loved beyond measure. Her heart constricted with the pain of Summer Sky's unhappiness. Her love for her little girl almost reached that of the man she had married.

She had wanted a better life for the two of them, only her limited options still posed the same problem. Summer Sky couldn't change her eye color, nor could her mother change the fact that she had married a white man. They must make the best out of the situation.

"Be brave Summer, while I clean the wound. This will hurt." Water Lily warned Summer Sky before she wiped the dried blood and dirt from the gash. The rock had delivered quite a wound just above her right eyebrow. She thanked God it hadn't hit her eye.

Her brave girl's breath hissed at inhale, but Summer Sky sat still as she tended the wound.

"This will need a couple of stitches. Do you recall what I use for numbing the skin? What would make this procedure more comfortable for you?" Water Lily asked her twelve-year-old daughter these types of questions often as she passed on her skills as a healer.

"Hmm, garlic water to clean the wound. You always have that around, right mama?"

"Yes, handy for all the scrapes and scratches you come back with." Water Lily smiled as she nudged her daughter under the chin with a chuckle. Summer Sky's smirk brightened the situation. But when those bullies mistreated her bright and kind daughter, her anger swelled.

Lord, help me put aside this anger at our situation, anger at Sam for leaving us. Help me keep my eyes on You.

"What else? What must I use as a poultice for its numbing effect?"

Summer Sky thought for a moment with her eyebrows scrunched together.

"Yarrow, but not the leaves. Is it the root?" She looked up.

"Well done, my smart little healer. But right now, I'll use Yarrow leaves. It'll stop the bleeding so that I can stitch you up. Hold this on your cut while I set tools out. You can name everything as I go." Water Lily set a tray on the table and added one thing at a time so Summer Sky could see them around the yarrow leaves she held onto her eyebrow.

"Astringent made from garlic kills germs, the special needle Papa bought you for making this task easier, thread made from the intestine of a porcupine." Summer Sky scrunched up her nose in such a way that she looked so much like her papa, it brought up bittersweet memories.

"What about this?" Water Lily took from behind her back a small jar of honey mixed with chamomile and willow bark tincture. She held up a spoon in her other hand. Summer Sky sighed and her shoulders slumped as if defeated. The honey worked to disguise the bitter flavor.

"Willow bark and chamomile for pain mixed with honey so that I will take it." She replied, then she drew her lips into a tight line, contradicting her willingness.

"That's my girl. Always willing to do what her mother asks of her." Water Lily opened the jar, filled the spoon, and held it for Summer Sky, her mouth opened like a baby bird.

"Mama, tell me about Papa." Summer Sky said out of the corner of her puckered mouth as she swallowed the large spoonful of sticky medicine.

With her heart still tender from her loss, even though she enjoyed talking about their past as much as her daughter loved hearing of it, Water Lily launched into the beloved story. She had told it from various moments in their years of knowing each other. This time, she began the story when she had met the dairy farmer from north of Newport. Then ended with the part where she loved, then married a man named Samuel and they had a beautiful daughter together with eyes as blue as a summer's sky.

"Well, let's see, your father brought us cheese and milk every week. I looked forward to his visit and would rush through my chores so I would have that much more time with him. My father thought I should become proficient with the English language and Samuel showed interest in learning Salish from me. I loved teaching him. I had never met anyone as wonderful as Samuel, smart and kind and so giving of himself. I would spend as much time with him as I could. Your father stood so tall and strong and when he smiled his whole face lit up."

"And he had blue eyes like me." Stated Summer Sky with pride in her voice.

"Yes."

"But the only blue eyes I have ever seen are mine. Why don't the Kalispel People have blue eyes?

"Well, most of us stay with our own people when choosing a mate. It's just simpler this way. Other cultures don't understand our way of life. Moving from Winter Lodge then Summer Village every year and living in our tipis instead of brick and wood houses. Staying put seems better for them. We think it's strange but it's not, only different."

"Have you ever met someone from your people with blue eyes like mine?" The hopeful expression on Summer Sky's face broke her heart. Then another set of blue eyes floated into the forefront of her memory.

"My grandmother, my mother's mother, had blue eyes. I had only seen her once or twice in my life because she lived in the State of Montana. The first time I saw her blue eyes they fascinated me, but hers had a greyer color, not as blue as yours. We tried getting our villages together in the summers, celebrating our heritage, but so many variables must fall into place.

"I thought the color of her eyes very strange yet wonderful at the same time. I remember her as a lovely and caring woman. She had a white father just like you. Maybe that's why I didn't feel strange about your father's blue eyes. And yours are even more wonderful, a gift from your father." Water Lily noticed the burn behind her eyes and if she thought on these things, tears may flow. Many years had passed since she cried from loneliness for her Samuel, she didn't want that kind of grief all over again.

She smiled and took a deep breath, then brough up the memory of holding her newborn baby girl. Pride and happiness replaced the ache. Ten long years without him, and someday she would see him again in heaven. That filled her heart with peace.

Summer Sky looked up at her with a smile.

"Mama, you got that remembering look again. Not a grievous remembering but quiet, as if you find comfort in the stories as much as I do."

Water Lily laughed aloud and hugged her very observant child.

"Sometimes you remind me of him. Like right now. Your father was a beautiful man, his heart especially. And he loved us so. He told me he fell in love the moment he saw me. He startled me while I harvested chamomile and strawberry leaves from the meadow near our summer village.

"I lobbed a rock at him because he scared me. He laughed so loud when the rock dropped several feet away from him. He said he could teach me how to throw like a man." Water Lily recalled the look that crossed Samuel's face as he said that. A little teasing, a little bit pink across his cheeks and neck as he stood in front of her with his hat in his hand. For the first time in her life, butterflies flitted in her tummy because of a way a man looked at her. But this part of the story she had always kept private.

Water Lily wanted that kind of love for her daughter, but her experience of both worlds made her wonder if Summer Sky's future would stay as alone as she had in her past. Because of her great love for Samuel, she would never love another, so at least she would continue supporting her daughter. They made a wonderful team.

Summer Sky cleared her throat, pulling Water Lily from her quiet thoughts.

"Where did you go, mama?" Her daughter smiled up at her with her wise eyes. She needed to finish her task while the story still distracted Summer Sky.

"The day I married him, I saw our little farm for the first time. Everything frightened me back then. I had never lived away from my father before. But he loved Samuel too, and it brought him happiness seeing his third daughter marry someone as good and kind as our Samuel."

Water Lily hesitated for only a moment and focused on the joy her husband had brought into her life instead of the loss.

"When we came around a stand of trees, there it stood on a hillside near a stream. My new home. It took my breath away, the stream glittered as it emptied into a small lake. Later, when I explored around the shore, I found cattails on the north end."

Water Lily stopped her movements and stared down at Summer Sky.

"What are cattails used for? All the parts." She asked her daughter while she put the first stitch in Summer Sky's numbed forehead.

"Umm, the dried seeds, named down, are like the soft under-feathers from ducks and are good for building fires when there are not enough coals. We also stuff pillows with the fluff or insulate our moccasins in the winter. "

Water Lily dabbed more numbing compound on her child's wound while she listened.

"The roots are good for food. Like a potato, but not as sweet. We make baskets by weaving the long grass like leaves. You can dry the core of the stalks and make arrow shafts. The pollen makes good flour, and we use it for thickening pea soup and venison stew. In spring we eat the new shoots on the roots, cooked or raw. The buds, too, before they turn brown and seedy are good. Like eating corn when it's young. The cattail is also used as medicine for wounds, burns, bruises, and stings. In so many ways they are quite valuable."

"Hmm, if you studied your reading as well as you have the cattail you would do better in school." Water Lily added another stitch.

"The cattail is an essential part of our daily lives, of course I would know everything about it."

All the time Summer Sky talked; Water Lily worked. Cleaning, preparing, and stitching.

"There, all done. It took four stitches. No one will even notice it once it heals. Now you must keep the stitches dry and stay away from those bullies."

Water Lily cleaned up and watched Summer Sky as she worked over something inside herself. Her thoughts flashing across her face seemed troubled and tumbled around as if in a wind.

"Papa has been gone a long time, has he not?" Before Water Lily could answer Summer Sky continued. "Even though I do not remember him, I am sure our lives would be happier if he were still with us. Especially for you, mama."

"This past summer you turned twelve, that makes ten years since Samuel passed away from getting kicked in the head by our plow horse." Water Lily stated with a flat voice. He hadn't come in for supper, and she found him lying face down in the stall.

"That thorn must have hurt something awful for the horse to have kicked Papa like that. I guess I am thankful it was only a rock that hit me and not a hoof from an angry horse."

With a heavy sigh, Summer Sky jumped off the table and joined her mother putting things away. Water Lily gathered her daughter into her arms and rocked her for just a moment, then watched as her beautiful, gentle, and strong daughter pulled away toward their fire ring, preparing their supper by the banked coals. Looking around their home Water Lily sighed too, she yearned for her hearth she shared with Samuel and Summer Sky in their little farmhouse by a lake. But instead, she saw a cozy haven where they shared every detail of their lives together.

CHAPTER THREE

Water Lily had sent Summer Sky out for the last of the season's yellow dock roots before the hard freeze took the plants to ground. That would make finding them much more difficult until late spring. She needed the distinct blossoms and seed stock to distinguish them from their toxic cousins. Her position depends on not poisoning the people who trusted in her care.

For an ample winter supply, she needed at least a basket or two more. In the winter months, Water Lily treated higher cases of indigestion from cured and dried meats. The lack of fresh fruit and vegetables didn't help either. Yellow dock purified the blood, and healed rashes and burns as well. She had learned this from her mother, like her mother before her, for generations. As a child herself, she disliked digging up these tough tubers. Lucky for Summer Sky, she used Samuel's metal shovel she had kept when they moved from the farm.

As Water Lily put her mending basket inside, she imagined herself at the little house by the winter-frozen lake. She and Samuel had stored up for the winter in the same way she and Summer Sky had, every year. They had spent the winter snuggled around the river stone fireplace planted in the center of their tongue and groove cedar farmhouse. The similarities stopped there. Nothing else would ever be the same.

She missed the warm utters and the gentle sounds of their milk cows. The joy of working beside her husband making cheese and butter and sour cream to sell in the nearby town store or delivering to their neighbors in exchange for eggs, meat, and grain. She missed her partner and the love she would never find again, not until heaven and eternity. She sighed.

She headed outside to tackle a new task. As Water Lily's hands moved through the familiar motions of strapping a stiff hide onto the stretcher frame, her thoughts shifted toward her warm and beautiful mother. As her hands moved as if on their own, she sifted through memories of gathering medicinal plants and roots with her in the summer-warmed fields. The sunshine slanted through the yellow leaves on the aspens along the creek nearby soothed the jagged corners of her heart. Water Lily learned about the healing herbs and remedies the same way she taught Summer Sky, through doing and seeing.

Water Lily found herself inventorying her supplies in her mind as she worked. This train of thought seemed more productive and safer. In the past, her grief for the loved ones who had passed took her down into a never-ending cycle of pain that could trap her forever if she let it. She focused on her daughter, filling her child with as much love as her past loved ones had poured into her. Only, for Summer Sky, making her life easier would require something she couldn't give her, her father back.

While Water Lily walked the trail of her past, she noticed her hands had rested on the elk hide she worked. She had bartered for it with her herbal remedies to replace the door flap. A spring windstorm had torn through a weak spot near the top strap that fastened the door to the frame of their tipi. Water Lily gauged with a practiced eye whether it would work for the old, shredded door. She had been so busy replenishing her winter stock she had finally gotten a chance to fix it.

Picking up the sharpened shale stone she used for separating the fibrous tissue on the underside from the skin, she resumed the slow and gentle task. She kept an eye out for Summer Sky, all the while watching over the other children, hoping they wouldn't bully her again so soon after the last episode.

Water Lily caught a glimpse of Summer Sky weaving her way through the village between the tipis. She stepped out from behind their neighbor's home with a heaping basket of roots. They stuck out like a pin cushion or a strange beast with many horns. Summer Sky's face shimmered with a sheen of sweat across her upper lip and chin.

She noticed the almost chestnut brown color she hoped for gathering this root so late in the fall. The perfect shade of brown peeked through the hairs and dirt still on the roots. These will become a potent batch of medicine.

"Heavy load?" Water Lily commented as Summer Sky plopped down beside her with a deep sigh.

"This ought to keep us well supplied for the winter. If it doesn't then I'll be surprised." Summer Sky dragged the kettle closer. They kept it warm near their outdoor firepit during the day. They found it easier to work on their projects in the fresh air and daylight than in the dark and sometimes smoky tipi.

Summer Sky poured hot water into a deep bowl used for washing, then scrubbed the small hairs off the roots with her dirty hands. Once she had gotten most of the loose soil off, she dipped them into the warm water with a look on her face near ecstasy.

"What's amiss, are your hands cold?" Water Lily held back the laughter at her daughter's dramatic antics, then with a snort, let loose her mirth at her funny girl.

"Not anymore." Summer Sky drew out another long sigh as she scrubbed the roots with her hands under the warm water's surface, then systematically trimmed and piled each root onto a tray they had hung on a stub where she had cut off a Fir branch above their work area.

Water Lily watched her daughter pour the muddy water out then take the empty kettle and bowl to the stream. She brought the kettle filled with fresh water and put it near the fire for later. Summer Sky grabbed a drying screen made of twigs from a young vine maple and laid out the long strips of yellow dock she had sliced.

"Will the hide cover the whole door without sewing pieces together like the patch worked one we made before?"

"It will make a nice door. Stronger than the last because you are right, it will be one piece. I haven't decided whether I will keep the fur on for added insulation or strip it off and decorate it." Water Lily's scraping and Summer Sky's slicing and chopping joined in their conversation like a well-played symphony of sound that comforted her soul. She had so much in life that filled her with gratitude, especially her most precious thing. The company of her beloved daughter. She would do anything for her within her power.

"I think we should decorate it with the sun again, but could we add things that I have learned since you painted the last one?" Summer Sky stopped her work and looked up with hope filled eyes.

"Hmm, tell me, what will accompany the sun on our door flap? What does the sun symbolize for our people?" Water Lily gave Summer Sky her full attention.

"The sun is our guiding light like the Holy Spirit God sent to comfort us?" Summer Sky looked away; it seemed as if she had become shy about sharing her idea.

"Hm mm, what else?" Water Lily smiled encouragement.

"The sun stands for good things like the sun rising every morning. And that there may be pain through the night, but joy comes in the morning. Terrible things come at us for a brief time, but it's fleeting. Like that rock and the stitches."

"Yes, that's true. You heal quickly. Where does that saying come from, joy comes in the morning?"

"The Book of Psalms, I think."

"Yes, Psalm Chapter thirty, verse five. It has comforted me through many a dark night."

Summer Sky unfolded her legs and stood, then bent down and lifted the full screen of sliced yellow dock roots, keeping it flat so nothing rolled off. She set it on a rack in the clearing just outside their tipi, out of the way and in the sunlight. Water Lily wondered if this batch would dry enough before the warm fall weather turned. She also noticed how long Summer Sky's legs had grown this past season. Soon she would become a young woman and no longer a child. "Back to the sun, is there more?"

"Hmm, sunlight reminds us of the Light of God so that the

darkness cannot overtake us. It gives its heat which warms the earth and grows food for our people so that we thrive.

"I will always want the sun symbol on our tipi, but something is missing and what I've learned from my father's bible is that I want Jesus there as well, but I'm not sure just what symbol to use. I didn't want to tell you because I'm uncertain. I thought you might chide me for not knowing. You may think I daydream while you read to me."

Summer Sky's ramble ended, but Water Lily could tell she held her breath. Water Lily held hers too. Could she admit to her daughter, who's faith and courage grew every day, could her own weak faith allow the bearing of Jesus' symbol on her very door, for all to see?

"There is time to talk about this more, I will need time to think…"

"And pray about it, right Mama?" Water Lily smiled and her heart lifted. Her daughter had her father's faith, and she silently sent a prayer of thanks to God for that. God had blessed Water Lily so much, her cup overflowed. She wanted to be brave enough to add the symbol of Jesus to her door, the cross He died on for her sins, declaring her love and faithfulness to Him.

"Hm mm, in the spring we'll have time to decorate it, but for now I'll just leave the fur on for added warmth. We have plenty of time to design a mural through the long winter months. Even beadwork, what do you think about that idea?"

"That's a wonderful idea." Summer Sky wiped her hands on a flour sack towel. She cleaned up the scraps of yellow dock scattered around their work area, throwing them in the fire with a sizzle.

CHAPTER FOUR

Someone had come for her mother, coughing. Summer Sky sat up. The fire smoldered with dull embers. The night visits from sick people needing her mother's help seemed routine.

"Go back to sleep, love." Water Lily whispered.

Summer Sky stretched and yawned what felt like only moments later. The lack of sound from outside confused her. She looked through the smoke hole and determined morning had come some time ago. She couldn't hear the usual sounds of people stirring, preparing for the day.

Her mother's sleeping furs lay empty. Summer Sky got up, grabbed some of last night's supper and set it on the near dead coals. Dressing while she waited for her breakfast, she worried about her mother and wondered why, she had never worried before.

She stepped out the door flap. The dark clouds and heavy air pressed down on her. As she walked into the center of their village toward the communal area, she noticed the firepit lay empty and cold. The hairs on the back of her neck tickled as they rose. Then she noticed the coughing.

She lit the fire and set the water to boil, she could do this at least.

Her mother pushed aside the wood-framed door of the Great Lodge.

"Summer, bring all our stock of willow bark, elderberry, balsam root and mustard-garlic paste. Oh good, you got water heating." Water Lily stood in the doorway, deep in thought, perhaps thinking of everything she needed. She looked tired; her mother had nursed the sick through the night.

"Hurry but leave all of it at the communal fire. Don't come near the Great Lodge, please honey. I need your help from over there. Do you understand?" Water Lily stared at Summer Sky as if to memorize her face. Then, she heard the coughing and crying coming from the Great Lodge. She turned, listening, people coughed and cried throughout the village.

"Yes mama, I understand. I'll hurry." Frightened, not even the bullies frightened her this much, panic flooded her heart. She ran as fast as she could toward their home on the outskirts of the village, slipping on the wet fall leaves slick with winter frost. Summer Sky threw open the tattered door flap of their tipi and charged into the storage area against the back of the one room. Mumbling the names of each herb, she stacked them on the worktable.

"Of course, willow bark, and strawberry root for sore throat. Oh yes, and the Yerba-Santa we got last summer from the travelers from Oregon, important medicine for the lungs. Hope we have enough." Summer Sky hesitated.

"Almost forgot, western hemlock and red cedar tea for congestion, and wild ginger to help sweat out the illness." Grabbing a basket, she could carry and with shaking hands, she worked fast. She tucked each vial inside, protecting them from breaking. Her urgent movements rattling the glass jars. She had helped pack twice a year for as long as she could recall, but not while people in her village lay sick.

Her mother waited for her, but she took the time, assuring she had everything before she hefted the basket onto her hip as she stepped through the doorway into the bitter wind that had picked up. It blew her hair in her face and slipped past the collar of her shirt. The soft days of a perfect fall had ended. Winter had come.

"Mama, I'm here." Summer Sky called out when she arrived at the communal fire and set down the basket. She stoked the fire, checked the large kettle, and found it boiling. She turned as she heard the door of the Great Lodge open.

"Start the willow bark steeping first, then run back and get our kettle." Her mother barked as she wiped off her hands with a rag. "Fill that one with strawberry root. Bring the pestle and mortar as well because I need poultices for at least ten people. I'm sure I have enough cloth for that many. Hurry, my love." Her mother smiled, but it didn't reach her grim face. She noticed a tightness in her mother's voice.

Summer Sky's hands flew through her work with a tenseness in her shoulders. She emptied the basket with frantic energy. Rushing back, she gathered the other things they needed.

She couldn't lift the full basket like she had done before. Grabbing the handle, she dragged it across the hard-packed clay floor then hefted it through the doorway. It wouldn't slide across the gravel on the trail. She searched for something she could place the basket on, then tow it across the ground.

"This might work." She yanked the elk hide off the stretching frame and left.

With the fur toward the gravel, she plopped the basket on top, then tugged. It moved better. Hunched over with the effort, puffing out thick clouds of breath in the chilly morning air, Summer Sky reached the central communal fire. The kettle steam mixed with her breath as she lifted the lid and checked its contents strength. She sniffed the willow bark tea and found it ready. The tea would help bring down fever inside the Great Lodge.

Taking their own kettle to the stream, she filled it. As she waddled her way along the trail with the heavy load, water sloshed onto her moccasins. She ignored the cold, stoked the fire on the other side of the pit and set up the second kettle. Summer Sky wondered if she could find a third. She would ask her mother.

In the past, working around the communal fire proved a privilege the few times Summer Sky joined her mother and the other women. They'd spread out their work and visited even through the winter months. Since they'd built the firepit with rock and hardened clay, the arm's length tall walls radiated warmth for several feet from its center. The cold only penetrated her winter clothes when she fetched more water at the stream.

"Mama, where could I find another kettle? I'll steep yarrow in it." Summer Sky asked when her mother stepped out of the Great Lodge for a breath of fresh air.

She looked at her mother when she didn't respond right away. Tears escaped and trickled down Water Lily's flushed cheeks. She wiped her face and took a breath then let it out.

"That's perfect, honey, helps break up congestion. I am proud of you, daughter. We will use Merri's kettle. She has no use for it," Water Lily said with little inflection in her voice.

The pain in her mother's eyes broke her heart. She watched her shoulders slump as she turned back toward the lodge and disappeared through the door. Merri had been her mother's best friend for as long as she could remember. Summer Sky sent up a prayer for her mother. She said a prayer for Merri and her family as she trudged toward another tipi that, perhaps, may never hear laughter again.

Sadness overwhelmed her as she threw open the door flap and entered Merri's home. Piles of rags on the floor told the story of Merri's frantic nursing of her family. Summer Sky resisted tidying the place, grabbed the kettle and rushed toward the stream for more water.

Water Lily came out of the lodge at predictable intervals throughout the day. Summer Sky anticipated the time with the next bowl of medicine, prepared and ready. They worked as one, an important part of their community. Pride surged inside her that she could help, however, she wished it hadn't happened this way with so many of their people sick.

Around midday, Summer Sky headed home to make food for her and her mother. They must keep up their strength. They would need it for battling the illness that had affected most everyone in their village. It seemed no one else could help her and her mother. She put a wrapped corn cake and a strip of venison near the door and stepped away. She ate her own meal while stirring the third kettle.

Water Lily came out, noticed the food, and slumped down against the wall of the lodge. Her mother's eyes drooped as if she couldn't keep them open. Summer Sky noticed her hair had slipped out of her braid. Several strands had come loose and stuck against her cheeks in the sweat that made her face shine.

"What else do you need, Mama? I could help you wash the faces with cool water."

"No." Water Lily barked at her in a surprising way she had never done before. Then a sad look came over her face.

"I'm sorry love, but I just don't want you to get sick. I need you too much and then I would worry about you. A fourth kettle would help, though. And thank you for keeping the buckets of water full. Thank you for thinking of that."

"I know what else I can do, Mama. I could pray for the people the way you taught me."

Summer Sky watched Water Lily's eyes fill with tears, and she blinked several times.

"Yes, honey, pray to our Father in Heaven for our people. Let's both pray non-stop until the sickness leaves our village for good."

"I will pray for you too, Mama, for courage and wisdom and strength to beat this sickness for our people."

"Amen, sweet girl, amen."

CHAPTER FIVE

As Summer Sky managed the fires and the kettles, all four of them, she waited with more medicine, and she prayed.

"Holy Father, I come for my mother's people. They need your help and healing. I pray for my mother; she needs your wisdom and strength. You are good and kind, and I thank you Lord for your son, Jesus. Amen."

At consistent intervals Summer Sky would hear someone scream in grief, and she prayed for the family of the soul that had passed on. But others had gotten better. The long week had dragged on since the arrival of the outbreak of what her mother called flu. Water Lily sat against the wall resting and eating. Summer Sky studied her mother's face which seemed drawn tight as if in pain. She searched for any sign of sickness. She looked tired but healthy. Summer Sky sighed with relief.

"Lord, protect my mother," she whispered. Summer Sky recalled the first time she had asked her mother why God had taken her father, knowing they needed him so much. Her mother replied that He worked in mysterious ways and His ways are not our ways. It seemed, at the time, a vague answer. She had never offered vague responses when Summer Sky asked her questions. Perhaps, her mother had sought the reason as much as she did.

Her mother had taught her God would never leave her nor forsake her. That comforted her, yet if God decided he should take her mother too, Summer Sky would have a tough time understanding why.

"I have never seen it this bad before. Those who have not gotten it have left the village. I worry that they are spreading it down the river in the other villages." Water Lily broke through Summer Sky's musings and rested her head against her bent knees. "I must focus on those who are left, though, for I have no power over what has already occurred." Water Lily commented while she ate as if she thought out loud.

Summer Sky heard a commotion in the lodge where the sick lay moaning. Both their heads pivoted toward the entrance. A grief filled shout forced through the wall of the building. Summer Sky and her mother scrambled onto their feet. One of the leaders pushed hard against the lodge door, it slammed against the wall not far from where Water Lily stood. He stomped toward her mother.

"This is all your fault." He spat at Water Lily inches from her face.

"How so, my brother?" She asked with her head down.

"This is a white man's sickness. You brought this upon us when you left us for that white man. None of us were good enough for you." He shook his fists near Water Lily's face. He growled, then turned and took his anger with him.

Not long after, they heard him groaning while things from his home clattered onto the gravel pathway. One after another, the items made a pile. The man stormed out the door with a saddle bag, every muscle in his face showed his control over the emotions raging inside him. He packed up his things, growling through clenched jaws, then flung the bag aside as he stomped toward them. Reaching into the communal fire, he snatched a burning log. Before they could stop him, he set his home on fire.

The reflection of the flames danced in his eyes as the fire and smoke engulfing his tipi, swirling into the winter gray clouds. Summer Sky prayed for him as he waited until the whole thing burned, then he walked toward the corral. A moment later, he galloped away with an eerie war cry on his lips.

"His grief said those words, Summer Sky. Do not judge him. I chose your father over him a long time ago. His wife died two days past, and his daughter must have just breathed her last. We must pray his grief won't consume him. And that he is not sick himself." Water Lily's shoulders slumped, and she dragged her feet as she walked back into the great lodge.

Summer Sky recalled that man's daughter. Raven. His daughter's kindness had shown through her eyes when the other children played elsewhere. When the bullies had surrounded her, Raven had stood back. Summer Sky had read the expression on the girls agonized face. It appeared Raven had wanted to defend the white man's daughter.

Summer Sky shared in Raven's father's grief. Large tears dripped off her chin and plopped on the back of her hand as she stirred the strawberry leaves and mint. She mourned the idea that she could have made friends with Raven if she hadn't had blue eyes. Then she cried for her father. The aroma of the strawberry leaves and mint filled her nose. She poured the remedy into a clean bowl, preparing it for the next person her mother would treat.

Long days turned into terrifying nights as Summer Sky slept under the hairy skin against the central fire pit. The warmth radiated from the wall of the pit and warmed her back. Cocooned in a world of comfort, peaceful sleep restored her strength, until pain-filled shrieks split the night. Another loved one had slipped from this world.

Her mother had taught her where God's people go. A heavenly place where God and Jesus lived, and they waited for her and Summer Sky. Her father waited there also since he loved Jesus too.

How many days had passed since that night when the coughing person had come for her mother's help? Fourteen days? Fifteen?

The sun neared the horizon when Summer Sky handed Water Lily the last of the willow bark tea.

"Mama, what else could we use?"

Her mother gazed at the bowl, quiet, then drank it down.

The bile churned in Summer Sky's gut. What would happen now that they had run out of medicine? Water Lily swayed in her exhaustion and sunk onto her knees.

"Mother!" Summer Sky raced toward Water Lily's side. She didn't care if she disobeyed her mother at that moment when she reached out for her.

"What can I do? What do you need?"

"I need sleep my love, just sleep. Help me up."

"But what about the others?" Summer Sky asked as she put her arm around her mother's waist and noticed her warmth. Too warm.

"There is nothing more I can do for them. They are gone now, Summer. All are gone now." Water Lily's legs buckled, but Summer Sky could take the weight, and this frightened her as well. Her mother's constant vigil beside the sick beds of her people had not only cost her sleep. Summer Sky slipped her arm around her mother's waist and gasped at how her ribs protruded through her doe skin dress. Too thin and too warm.

"Gone?" Summer Sky hesitated, fearing the truth.

"Gone to heaven or gone away." Water Lily explained, shuffling toward home.

They reached their tipi as the last of the rays of the sun left the western horizon. Once inside, Summer Sky realized they hadn't been home for a long time. The cold had seeped into everything. They hadn't had a fire for so long she must fetch a stick from the communal fire.

"Mama, lie down and rest. I will take care of you now." Summer Sky pulled cattail fluff and small strips of cottonwood bark from a wood box they kept at one edge of their storage. She piled it in the middle of the cold fireplace, laid several layers of kindling over it but left a hole like cave in the structure, then ran to the communal fire that still blazed.

Pulling the kettle from the iron arm it hung on, she peered in, praying for enough medicine for her mother. About a knuckle's worth sloshed on the bottom which would give at least one dose, maybe two. She grabbed the end of a stick that hadn't burned all the way and waited, hoping it would stay lit, then hooked the kettle with the other hand and headed back.

Summer Sky watched the stick as she walked, slowing her steps when the air current from her movements threatened to extinguish the tiny flame. She reached their home and backed in through the door flap, careful with the glowing stick. Setting down the kettle she crouched in front of the stacked kindling and set the stick in it. It flared and acted like it would go out, but then caught the flame and chased the darkness from their round home.

The smoke rose toward the top of the tipi and slid silent into the night, as if nothing in their world had changed. But the village had changed, forever. The eerie silence throughout the once thriving community overwhelmed her. The insidious sickness had stolen so much.

In a frantic, panicked moment, Summer Sky scrambled in her mother's direction. She reached out and touched her. Relief flooded through her when Water Lily made a quiet sleeping sound.

Determined to save her mother from the fever, Summer Sky lit an oil lamp and set it on the workbench. Her mind ran through every lesson her mother had taught her about natural medicines they had gathered and prepared through the years, as far back as her memories went. But the shelves lay bare.

Summer Sky ran to the communal fire, and with the last of the light and heat it radiated, packed up the remaining jars of herbs into the cattail basket. She checked the other kettles, pulling them one at a time, bone dry. Taking one in each hand, she refilled them in the creek, then hung it over the fire, stoking it hot again. Once she had enough hot water she would wash the death off her mother from head to toe, including her hair.

Illness will not grow where there is fresh air and cleanliness, Summer. She could hear her mother's teaching.

Summer Sky organized the woodpile at the communal fire then hefted the basket, testing the weight, unhappy with what it lacked. Yes, not much remained of their stock of medicines.

CHAPTER SIX

For days, it seemed weeks, her mother lay in her sleeping furs and couldn't get up. Summer Sky persuaded her with cool fresh water for her parched throat. She spooned water into her mother's mouth, then runny oats mixed with dried wild strawberries, giving her sustenance. Her mother's breathing labored. With each breath the tendons on her neck stood out like thick ropes.

She pushed away every thought of losing her and combed through her brain. Could she have gaps in her education? Even though their stock had diminished, they must have other herbs that would help. Replenishing their supplies must wait until spring and summer. Yet perhaps she hadn't learned everything she needed.

"Momma, what have I missed? What have I forgotten? Is there something I haven't tried?"

"No, honey, you're a good student. You have learned enough. My body has gotten too tired. I'm so sorry, Summer." Her mother's shoulders bounced as she sobbed, tearless. The fever had dried her up. She needed more fluids... maybe the sweat lodge would help. If she could get her there then she could pour fluids into her as she released the illness.

"Momma, the sweat lodge. We can sweat out this sickness. I will keep the fire going, and you can just get better." Summer Sky had heard her mother advise others about the benefits of the sweat lodge for many things, including helping them recover when the flu had hit in times past.

"No, don't go in there, Summer. Promise you won't go in there. In fact, set flame to the sweat lodge and the Great Lodge. Don't go in. There's no one left still alive but us." Water Lily struggled into a sitting position, and Summer Sky reached for her.

"Yes, mother. Take deep breaths. Try."

The intake of air brought on a fit of coughing. Deep and dry, the rattling evident in the breaths her mother took. Water Lily sighed after the coughing subsided.

"Then once that's done, I will tell you what we will do next."

Summer Sky torched the buildings even though it broke her heart. The great illness had changed their lives forever. Despite the bullying, which she hated; she had loved their home on the river. Where would they go now?

When Summer Sky finished that dreadful deed, the stench of illness and death turned the sky black. She watched with tears dripping off her chin, reminiscing on every day she had witnessed in this community and the connection she had with her mother there. How would the world acknowledge the People here?

She promised herself she would somehow memorialize her mother's people.

I will think about that later, she thought as she headed home. When she stepped through the door, she found her mother stuffing Summer Sky's belongings into the travel bags that strapped across the rump of her horse.

"What are you doing? Are we leaving?"

"You're leaving. You will follow the river north to my brother's village." Water Lily dragged a cattail basket from under the work bench and placed the remaining remedies into it, one at a time.

"We need these to get you better first." Summer Sky took the things back out as her mother put them in, struggling with a panic brought on by what her mother had said.

Water Lily grabbed her hands in a strong grip, which surprised her, for being so sick. Didn't that prove her mother had gotten better?

"Maybe there's still time to help them overcome this

illness. You must go."

"I won't leave you."

The look on Summer Sky's face must have seemed so compelling that Water Lily softened. She sat, but landed hard, on the floor near the hearth as if her legs were not bones, muscle, and sinew but cattail fluff.

"In a few days then." Water Lily boiled water like any normal morning.

They sat in silence and drank their tea together. Summer Sky swam in her own thoughts. Her chest gripped with a sense of foreboding. There must be something she could do, something more. She prayed a silent prayer, begging God to spare the only person left that loved her. She gazed at her mother across the fire pit, assessing, and could not find what she looked for. The hope that her mother would get better her only thought, blocking out all other scenarios.

Water Lily slumped as if she couldn't hold herself in a sitting position any longer. She crawled back under her sleeping furs. Summer Sky pulled her mat near her mother's and watched the sun's progress as it drew a stark line on the inside of their home. From late afternoon and into the evening, she lay beside her mother and prayed.

Summer Sky weaved her fingers with her mothers, pleading for her recovery. She became the comforter, reciting the story of Water Lily's great love, Samuel. She spoke of the birth of their beautiful baby girl with eyes as blue as the summer sky.

She held her mother's hand through the night. By morning, Water Lily's hand had grown as cold as the ash in a dead firepit.

CHAPTER SEVEN

"It's morning, Mama." Summer Sky rubbed her mother's cold hand, willing warmth back into it. She had left her hand outside of her sleeping furs all night. She rubbed it with no response. She must wake up to take more medicine. Summer Sky yanked her arm. The coldness of her mother's hand sent a chill deep into her stomach, gripping it with sickening fear. "Mama, wake up."

The foreboding from the day before became a full-fledged beast inside her chest. With her breath catching in her throat, Summer Sky flung the sleeping furs off Water Lily's body. She laid her hand over her mother's heart, then her wrist, feeling for a heartbeat, searching, and praying for any sign of life. She lay with her ear on her mother's cold chest, as cold as her hand. Understanding and yet not understanding warred in her head. This could not happen. Her mother couldn't leave her. Why would God do this to her? No, he must take her too or bring her mother back.

"Give her back, Lord. You can do that. But if you want her with you in heaven then take me too… God, please."

Summer Sky sat up and stared at the lifeless body. Water Lily's face had a peaceful expression, as if she would open her eyes at any moment. She stared for what seemed like hours. Her mother's labored breathing, gone. Her struggle to stay with Summer Sky, over. She couldn't have died. She wouldn't leave her, not ever.

"No, please, Mama come back." Summer Sky whispered as she grasped two handfuls of her mother's night dress. She buried her face in the soft cotton and sobbed. She lifted her eyes and searched for life again, willing for continued denial. The emptiness hit Summer Sky so hard it took the breath out of her in a woosh of air.

"Mother? What will I do without you?" She couldn't breathe. Grasping her throat, her burning lungs begged for air. Panic found her knocked off balance and she landed on her rump. She gasped for air and scrambled onto her knees, collapsing over her mother. A piercing wail came from the depths of Summer Sky as the thought of her aloneness shattered her resolve.

"Mama, take me with you. I can't do this on my own." Desperation overrode her thinking. Summer Sky shook her mother again and again.

"What will become of me? Please, come back."

Summer Sky plopped onto her sleeping mat and pulled her legs up under her chin. She wrapped her arms around her knees, rocking. She searched for comfort in the movement. Her mind whirled around all the obstacles she could see of her future. Her mother had trained her as a valuable contributor in the village, yet the glaring truth had remained, mistrust. Mistrust of her white father's blood, something she had no control over. Summer Sky's mistrust because of the poor treatment she had endured throughout her life.

What should she do? Her mother had wanted Summer Sky to join her uncle's village, but she wouldn't belong there either. Her bright blue eyes, a glaring example of how she would never fit into what the others wanted of her. Brown eyes, not blue. A native father and not Samuel Bishop.

Sunlight slipped through the smoke flap and fell over Summer Sky's face reminding her of the time. The morning had escaped into the afternoon. The time surprised her. It seemed only moments ago that she had awoken and found her mother gone. But hours had passed. She must do something. She could not sleep another night with her mother's body still with her. She must bury her, but where?

If only she knew the location of her father's grave. They

should rest near each other. Because of her faith, she understood her mother's soul had joined her father in heaven and that gave her grief a slight reprieve.

Summer Sky stood stiff from sitting for so long, her leg tingled. Snagging the kettle off the cold firepit, she limped from the tipi toward the stream. She must eat and keep herself together.

Standing in the afternoon sun on the early winter day, she couldn't balance the beauty of the river with the turmoil in her heart. The frost still glistened on the northern side of the trees where the sun had not reached. She couldn't reconcile the sparkling view with so much death and the fact that everyone had left her.

Why had she not gotten sick along with the others? Had her mother protected her from the worst of it? Questions swam through her thoughts as she slid onto her knees among the rounded pebbles on the edge of the stream. The frigid water washed over her hand once the kettle filled. The stark cold of it reminded her of her mother's still body.

She must do something with her mother. She must bury her, but where? And could she do it herself? With the agony of isolation palpable in her chest, she gripped the front of her doe skin dress. She understood now why someone deep in grief would cut their hair off and scrape their nails down their arms until they bled, as an outlet for their pain. Her mother would treat their wounds and talk with them about a loving God who would bring them peace someday.

But at that moment as Summer Sky found her way through the homes of the lost, her faith in God hadn't drawn the pain out but slammed it into her afresh. She dropped and slid onto her face as fresh tears spilled on the frosted grass.

"Why did you not save my mother? Why did you take her and not take me too?" She cried out to God in her rawness, and in her tormented soul she found nothing but painful loss.

Why couldn't she save the one person that meant life and death to her. Guilt and shame flushed her frigid face warm.

Maybe if she had studied harder and longer, then she would have known what she had missed. Her hands dug into the turf, ripping handfuls of it from the frosty soil. Anger built in her gut, anger at herself, for her failures. She fought against making decisions without her mother.

Why should she? She was only twelve years old. She still needed her mother. How could this have happened?

"God, how will I do this alone?" Summer Sky screamed her denial into the damp grass against her cheek. Her heart, painful and broken, so much so she found breathing difficult. She pushed away from the ground onto her hands and knees. Her breath catching, a great keening boiled out of her soul. She screamed until she had nothing left.

She rolled onto her back and watched the cattail-fluff clouds skitter across the blue sky in a hurry. They understood their path, more than she. She watched as one after another raced each other and gathered on the horizon. Summer Sky sat up in a panic. She must decide where to bury her mother and soon. A storm brewed.

She slipped inside her home and found her father's old shovel. Digging in the frozen ground this time of year would prove a challenge, but she must try. With a stronger resolve, Summer Sky headed uphill away from the creek where she and her mother enjoyed warm spring mornings basking in the sun in the little meadow just above their home. She hoped the last few days of sunshine might have softened the ground enough.

As she dug into the earth, she thanked God for being with her, and for the physical exertion granting her a reprieve from the pain. She had never dug a grave before. Tradition had tasked the male leader of the family with this responsibility. So much of Summer Sky's life had not fit into the norm. She couldn't fathom someone else helping her. She had no one left.

She gathered the big rocks she dug out of the pit and set them apart from the dirt. She scanned the sky for the storm she had seen, but it must have taken pity on her for the sake of her mission.

"Thank you, God," she whispered as she placed another big rock onto the growing pile with the others.

Her labored breath blew out from her in billows of clouds into the air, as she dislodged the dirt with her spade, filled the shovel, then threw it over her shoulder to the edge of the grave, then down for another shovel full. The cadence of her work numbed her mind.

She stood, judging her progress. With the needed break, Summer Sky leaned on the handle of the shovel and imagined removing her mother's body once she found her father's grave and placing them together. Any deeper would make it that much harder to bring her mother back out. The pile of rocks she accumulated would almost cover the grave. She would carry more from the river.

Summer Sky panicked anew when she saw the angle of the sun. She had less than two hours before it set. Hurrying down the hill toward her tipi she whistled for her horse. Weeks had passed since she had given Wind her attention, she hoped he wouldn't hold that against her. She stopped and waited when she heard the thundering of hooves from the river. Wind stopped ten feet in front of her and chuffed a greeting. Summer Sky wondered if Wind could smell death on her.

"You're alright. Come here Wind. I need your help." Summer Sky reached her hand out, but she didn't move closer. She understood that he must decide for himself and come on his own. Wind blew out a puff of steam into the late afternoon air as he lowered his head and ambled over toward where Summer Sky stood. He put his warm nose into her outstretched hand.

"That's a good boy." Summer Sky leaned into her horse's face and their foreheads met. She breathed in his grass smell and almost crumbled with the weight of what she must do. She gripped Wind's tangled mane and balanced herself, keeping from falling on her knees again. She had no time left for grief.

"Come on, boy, we have something important we must do." Summer Sky swung herself onto Wind's back and steered him with her legs toward the tipi. She pulled two of the poles from opposite sides of their tent home and attached them onto Wind's travois harness, then she fastened the skin bed on the other end that slid along the ground. She would place her mother there and the travois would carry her. But first she must sew her grave clothes.

Working as fast as she could, she wrapped her mother in the layers of her bedding and tied every angle, every flap, every bend secure, keeping the elements at bay, perhaps forever. Summer Sky could not predict what her future held, where she may land once this illness cleared.

Pulling Water Lily through the door flap and onto the travois exhausted her muscles but Summer Sky could not focus on their screaming pain. She had done the work of two grown men. She tied her precious cargo on the bed of the travois, protecting her mother for the climb up the hill toward the meadow. Summer Sky tried jumping onto Wind's back but couldn't with the little amount of strength she had left so she walked beside him.

As they reached the site, Wind shied away from the gaping gravesite for a moment before she caught him around the neck, comforting him and herself. Another plea went from her lips for courage as she slid her body into the oblong hole and with gentle hands pulled her mother into her aching arms. Summer Sky's throat closed with the pain of her loss as she looked down at the small form at her feet. She had always thought her mother was much bigger than that.

Grabbing the side of the travois, she pulled herself from the earth then shoved the dirt back into the hole while great drops dripped from her chin and fell onto her hands making a muddy mess. She didn't care anymore. She cared little about anything anymore. She asked God that when this day ended, she wouldn't wake up to a new one.

Once Summer Sky had run out of dirt, she stacked the rocks on top of the grave. The rocks would protect the site from predators, but she would need more.

An icy gust rattled the naked branches on the deciduous

trees surrounding the meadow. Summer Sky shivered; the exertion had dampened her clothing through with sweat trickling down her neck into her coat. The rest of the rocks would wait.

Pulling Wind next to a downed tree, she climbed upon his back. Her stomach growled, reminding her she hadn't eaten all day. She must change out of her wet clothing, eat something, and then rest. She laid along her warm friend's back and sighed.

"Let's go home, Wind." She closed her eyes and rocked back and forth with the motion of her horse as he navigated through the trees with the empty travois still attached. Summer Sky stroked the soft thickening winter fur around her chestnut gelding's neck, drawing comfort. When the motion stopped, she didn't want it to end. She pried herself away from the cocoon of warmth and love she and her horse had created.

When she slid off Wind's back and landed on her feet, she groaned from the pins and needles. Her frozen feet shot pain up her legs. She had no way of getting warm. She hadn't lit the fire that morning. Tears of frustration and exhaustion slipped from her eyes. She wiped them away as they came. Wisdom told her more moisture would make her that much colder. Her anger at herself for crying like a baby shocked her.

Her responsibilities weighed heavy upon her. She took the harness from Wind's back and patted him on the rump. She had done this since he became hers. Her signal he could go, but he didn't leave. He just bumped her with his head until she wrapped her arms around him and held on tight.

"I must get inside. I can't stay with you right now." Summer Sky pulled away from him and slipped inside. As she gathered cattail fluff and bark shavings, Summer Sky took her flint out of a pouch that hung from a peg on the wall. Making fire took time so she changed out of her wet and dirty clothes first.

She poured a glass of water from the kettle and gulped it down, then poured another. She chided herself for not doing better as she settled into the laborious process of creating fire when the fire had gone out.

CHAPTER EIGHT

Startled, she listened for what had disturbed her from a deep sleep so well needed. Her breath quiet as she trained her hearing past the crackling fire. A cold draft found its way under the ripped door flap, prompting a tug on her sleeping fur, tucking it tighter around her neck.

Summer Sky sat up. She heard something scratching at her door. Through the smoke hole snowflakes filtered and mingled with the sparks from her fire. A gust of wind pushed hard against the side of her tipi. She may need those two poles she had used for the travois before the storm ended. She had left them outside in her rush to warm herself.

More scratching, then a nose poked through the bottom. Summer Sky grabbed a half-burned stick and raised it up in defense. She kept an eye on the door while she reached for her bow and quiver of arrows, but she'd left them against the wall out of reach. Then, a familiar sound came from the intruder.

"Wind, you scared me. What are you doing?" Summer Sky opened the door and greeted her friend, as he pushed himself into her home. Having the big animal inside emptied the space of room. She reached for him, and her hand scraped across a thick coat of ice on Wind's shoulder that dripped once the warmth from the fire hit it.

"Cold out there boy? Come on in then, make yourself comfortable." The antics of her horse, doing something she had never seen a horse do, tickled her. She pulled him the rest of the way in and made him lay down in the empty space on her side of the tipi. Her sleeping mat had remained near her mother's.

"We will wait out the storm together, my friend." Summer

Sky did her best to secure the door flap and threw another armload of wood she had stacked against the wall, into the flames. The warmth spread, and Wind shivered.

The dilemma struck Summer Sky as odd. During storms all the horses headed into the trees and stood together for warmth and protection. Had the other horses run for shelter in the trees? Why had Wind not gone with them? Then it hit her. He must have sensed her despair and refused to leave her alone.

She took a wool blanket and covered her shivering horse. She sat and leaned against him as she rubbed his legs with a dry deer skin rag, cleaning the melting snow and ice off him. He knocked her with his big head in thanks, and she shoved him away laughing. Laughter, it seemed like a foreign sound coming from her lips. She couldn't recall the last time she had laughed. Weeks?

Warmth from Wind radiated through the blanket, and it comforted her.

"Come morning, you and I must decide where we will go. But now I'm still too tired." Summer Sky reached for another one of the oatcakes she had made earlier and broke it in half, offering Wind the other piece. He nibbled on the oatcake then licked the crumbs off her hand.

"That's a bit disgusting, Wind." Summer Sky blurted as she drew her hand back and rubbed it on the blanket covering her horse. He nickered a soft response and bumped her again.

With the extra warmth from her large friend in her living quarters, Summer Sky's eyelids drooped. She stoked the fire and banked a generous portion of the embers for morning.

She drank the last of her cold tea she hadn't finished the evening before and crawled into her sleeping furs. She peered out across the fire at her dear friend and met his eyes.

"Thank you, Wind, for staying with me." She said as tears filled her eyes, blurring everything around her.

"Thank you, God, for Wind." She smiled and closed her eyes with a sigh.

CHAPTER NINE

Wind's soft nose tickled Summer Sky's face, and her eyes popped open. His behavior, coming in from the storm the night before, warmed her heart.

"Thank you, Lord, for my dear friend."

The storm had stopped pushing against the walls of her home. The foul weather had passed. She looked through the smoke hole. With the lack of sunshine, she couldn't determine the time of day, grey clouds filled her view.

Once Summer Sky stirred, her guest headed for the door.

"Alright, hold on, I'm coming." Summer Sky pushed her warm sleeping furs aside and shivered. The bitter morning air bit at her skin through her night dress. Once she had untied the door flap, Wind pushed around her and slid through the door. He squeezed through, the top of the opening sliding across his back as he walked out.

Putting on her long moccasins and fur lined leggings under her night dress cut the chill. She sifted through the ash in the fire pit and piled glowing coals together. Soon, the fire blazed.

Her warm bed tempted her. She could crawl back in, block out the world and all the harsh realities that filled it. Yet her reality forced her into the day. She must leave, the sooner the better.

She struggled into her parka and stepped outside. The frost-saturated air tickled the hairs inside her nose. Despite the lack of sunlight, she shielded her eyes from the brightness of the snow until they adjusted. The minimal light bounced off the snow crystals and refracted until everything in her sight sparkled. The snow covered the village in pristine white, yet it dampened her enthusiasm. She hadn't planned for this nuisance. The cold and the amount of snow would make leaving that much harder.

Before she had drifted off to sleep the night before, Summer Sky had decided she would never live in her uncle's village. Without her mother's protection, she could not put herself through even the possibility of the same treatment. And, without her mother, everything seemed that much more overwhelming.

She had two options and must choose one. Find where her father had lived and learn about his side of her family history or accept a life by herself with Wind. She leaned toward living her life alone.

But she must find a place where no one could find her. Not her mother's people nor her father's people. As soon as word reached her uncle of the sickness in their village, he would come for his sister. If he had lived through the epidemic.

Summer Sky walked to the stream, filled her kettle, thinking about which direction she would go.

Get thee up into the high mountains.

A peace and warmth spread throughout her body.

"Thank you, Father." She praised God for His comfort.

The decision made; she would head up.

As she walked back, she realized something. No one would look for her. No one would even think she had survived the outbreak. She stood at her door wondering why the revelation failed to give her more peace. Sorrow crouched at the edge of her mind with the awareness of her isolation. She pushed the grief to the back of her mind while she ate a chunk of smoked salmon on an oat cake.

After breakfast she whistled for Wind, and he came along with her mother's mare. Another horse changed things. She could bring two travois and scrounge through the village for anything else she may need.

She first packed the inside of the tipi onto her mother's

golden blond palomino, Sunshine. Then she took the outer and inner layers of the tipi off the pine poles, the frame of her dwelling. She broke down her work bench the same way she and her mother had done so many times and stacked the pieces near the pile of household items she would organize once she got the poles down. The poles posed a problem for just one person, but she would make do. As she pulled on a pole, the rest toppled in her direction like giant match sticks. She jumped out of the way and landed on her backside in the snow. With a huff, she pushed herself off the ground and dusted the snow off her clothes and hands.

She wrapped the poles with the walls and attached them to Wind as the second travois.

Summer Sky had made a mental list of the things she would scavenge. The most important item, a replacement door flap. She wandered the vacated village looking for what she wanted and found it at her chiefs' door. Should she dare? She stared at it for what seemed a long time but decided against it. The last thing she needed, someone coming across her lone camp and misunderstanding her intentions.

She kept looking. But when she came across Merri's home, the stabbing pain in her heart stopped her. The intricate beadwork of blue sky, white fluffy clouds, and big rays of the sun reminded her so much of her mother. It would honor her memory every time she went through it.

Once she had untied the flap and had stripped it from the frame, she entered the home. The quiet place made Summer Sky's knees shake from the spooky thought that her mother's best friend had passed. To her it seemed as if she had trespassed on sacred ground, but she set that thought aside.

Merri wouldn't mind if she took the things she needed. She must prepare for long term and gather more bedding and clothing, including an extra parka in case hers got wet. Merri had a beautiful fur-lined hooded parka. Summer Sky recalled Merri and her mother working on it together around the communal fire just before her friend's wedding.

She scrounged for food in the rest of the village since no one else remained. Surprised by how little she had found; she packed the items onto the two travois and wondered at the scarcity of food. Had the men planning on the hunting getting them through the winter? They must have.

Which didn't bode well for Summer Sky. Her arrows fell short of the target and always landed on the left. In the past the warriors had kept she and her mother stocked in exchange for their medicinal treatments. What would she do now?

She had found a few bags of oats, one bag of wheat flour, dried corn in a basket, and two baskets of dried venison. Placed with the food from her home, she could make it stretch for a month. When she torched the main lodge, she had concluded a good portion of their winter stockpile had gone up in flames with it. Nothing she could do about that now.

She leaned against Wind's shoulder and looked around one last time at the Winter Village along the edge of the Pend Oreille River. The communal fire, where her mother had needed her, sat cold and empty of kettles and the iron arm. She had packed them with her things on one of the travois. The blackened frames of the Great Lodge and the Sweat Lodge behind it haunted her. Summer Sky glanced at Raven's home, the girl who she could have built a friendship with, the half-burnt poles stood like a skeleton, reminding her of the final decision to live alone. All this brought back the pain of her terrible loss. Burying her face in her horse's neck, Summer Sky said good-bye. Damp trails sliding, searing hot, down her frozen face.

Because of the new snow and the loaded down horses, Summer Sky led them through the abandoned village while using her snowshoes. She had one stop before they could go, she must say good-bye to her mother. Once she had placed the last of the rocks onto her mother's grave, Wind gave a neigh of approval as his load lightened. Instead of scrounging for rocks at the river she gathered what she'd needed from abandoned hearths, including her own.

They left the area in the early afternoon and traveled into

the mountains east of the river. Without the cover of her warm tipi, tonight she'd sleep in the open. She judged the clouds above her, praying for mild weather while she searched for her new home.

CHAPTER TEN

Summer Sky gauged the angle of the sun. They had traveled a few hours. Because of the short days of winter, they needed shelter for the night soon. They had climbed uphill from the river and through every type of terrain; steep side hill, rolling hill, forests, and rocky cliffs.

A nice rock outcrop with an overhang would work for the night, and Summer Sky scanned the white environment. The sun showed itself at the edge of the horizon. She had little time before darkness inhibited her movements. She headed in a direction that gave her the most promise.

Summer Sky stopped at the base of a cliff and scuffed her snowshoes around in a circle. The cliff didn't have a place that qualified for a roof of any kind but if she leaned the poles against it and covered them with the skins, it could work. She led Wind alongside the wall and unlatched his load first, then she did the same with Sunshine.

The horses frolicked together, rolling in the snow. A smile forced its way through Summer Sky's grief for just a moment, then she turned toward her makeshift camp site. She needed firewood and water, but nothing in her view indicated a water source. Throughout the mountains and forests, she had visited many lakes with her mother, but they hadn't foraged in this area.

"Mother, am I doing the right thing?" Summer Sky whispered as she scanned the vast, unfamiliar terrain. The deepening sunset begged admiration but her doubts about her decision to live alone overwhelmed her. Go forward, turn back. She spun around and studied their tracks in the dim light as her heart clattered against her ribs. The expanse of snow and trees and mountains intimidated her.

What makes you believe you can succeed? You will die out here and no one will care.

The voice in her head sounded a lot like the taunts she had grown up with and she must fight against them. She couldn't give in, or she might lose her mind. She might lose her fortitude that held her courage in place. The courage she needed to stand and not fall in the snow and let it take her life. She could not entertain these thoughts.

"God will care." She said out loud in a defiant manner, shutting out the bully. She straightened her back and repeated it louder. "God is with me. He will not forsake me." A sigh escaped her lungs and her body relaxed, free of anxiety. The mean-spirited voice, silenced.

With the bout of fear dealt with, clarity returned, and she saw what she needed. On the edge of the field of snow, an aspen grove stood. Aspens grew best in wet ground. She pulled the big fur her mother had chosen for a new door and headed in that direction.

As Summer Sky snowshoed down the winter covered slope, she thought about the fur and how she might use it. The fur helped her gather more at one time instead of making several trips. She could fashion a harness for over her chest instead of pulling with her arms. Somewhat like the harness on the travois.

Summer Sky made quick work of bringing out enough dry aspen wood lying under the snow in the stand of trees and looked for water. If a stream ran through the grove, the winter cold had frozen it solid. Grabbing the two corners of the fur she yanked, but it wouldn't budge. She blamed the heavy load. She had put the fur side down the same way she had over the gravel. Why wasn't it easy like before? Frustrated, she lifted one corner and studied the matted snow on the hairs. She swiped at it and realized she had pulled against the grain. Like petting a horse against the natural direction the hair grew. She yanked the other side of her load, and it broke free. In fact, it moved with very little effort. Summer Sky made her way across the clearing and dumping her pile of wood in just a few minutes. She had learned a valuable lesson about her new fur sled.

At the base of the cliff wall, piles of broken rock had sluffed off the face through the years. She stacked them on one side for a firepit and low wall, keeping the warmth centered under her makeshift shelter. She dug around for her fire kit and pulled out her kettle, frying pan, cornmeal, and dried venison.

Once she had laid her cattail fluff and bark shavings, she snapped off small twigs from the branches in the pile and laid them across the tinder. She dug a flint out of her bag. She hoped it would ignite on the first try but it didn't. Strike after strike, with each strike of her flint she adjusted her angle and fire materials. Many variables went into a fire. Moisture in the twigs, a probable problem. She protected her cattail fluff in her waterproof pouch. If a strong wind blew, it could blow out the tiny flame before it had ignited the kindling. Though cold, the air seemed stagnant without the slightest breath of wind.

It took ten strikes with the flint, then a big spark dropped into the cattail fluff and smoke curled through the twigs. Another strike, a gentle blow and she got a flame. She fed it with more twigs, then she snapped small branches in half using her knee. Next, she scooped up a kettle of snow. She used some water from the pouch she carried under her coat keeping it from freezing and primed the snow. If she didn't put water into the snow, it would take much longer for it to melt. She had no idea why, only that it worked. Her uncle had taught her this trick as she sat near him so long ago, before her mother had become the healer of a new village.

While she waited, she took out the dried venison and laid some in the frying pan along with a few pinches of wheat flour. She poured a small amount of the melted snow from the kettle over it. She wished for some root vegetables but the minimal amount she'd gathered remained buried in the packed travois. She would make do.

Once Summer Sky had eaten dinner, she made a batch of

oat cakes for tomorrow. As the sun broke out of the clouds on the horizon, she made a second trip across the meadow for enough wood for the night.

Wind and Sunshine came back just after dark and settled in near the light of the fire. The sight of them comforted her. She burrowed deeper into the sleeping furs she had laid out under the makeshift roof. Staring at the fire, despair niggled at her heart.

"Mama, I miss you." Summer Sky sniffled. The burning behind her eyes a telltale sign of her grief but she shoved it aside. She must stay focused on the journey and finding her new home. She must stay focused on her Savior who will help her through.

"Thank you, Lord, for your comfort and your provision."

CHAPTER ELEVEN

Summer Sky rolled over, relieving her ribs from the rock under her bed roll. Making a hasty shelter the evening before hadn't given her time to clear the rocks from under the snow. Her body heat had melted the snow and the rocks had made her night's sleep impossible.

She sat up. Wind lifted his head and chuffed a greeting. The first hint of morning light made the horse's silhouette discernable against the dark western sky. At this time of year, she estimated the sun would rise soon.

With a stick from her diminished stack of wood, she stirred the ash searching for embers. Gathering the glowing charcoal into the center of the makeshift fire pit, Summer Sky placed small sticks on them and blew. Soon, she had a flame without much effort.

"Easy. Hope the rest of the day goes as well."

Summer Sky stacked on larger pieces of wood, feeding her fledgling flames. She reached for her pot and went in search of clean snow. She noticed Sunshine hadn't joined them. She whistled her special tune for the horses and waited. Wind followed her with his head down bumping her with a morning greeting. Summer Sky's gut churned with fear from what Wind communicated. Away from the bright glow of the fire, her eyes adjusted in the predawn light bouncing off the snow, changing the greys, black and white, and then more discernable shapes with every second that ticked by.

With the cliff facing west, Summer Sky readjusted her calculation of the time as the sun burst through the sporadic trees at the top of the cliff. The brilliant rays bathed the small meadow before her in sparkles, taking her breath away. Pink, orange and subtle hews of lavender spread over the shadows between the birch trees at the edge of the snow-covered meadow.

Then she heard it. Was this what Wind had warned her about? She stopped moving. Holding her breath, she listened, deciphering the cause of the sound. Scratching. Scuffling. Panting.

She caught a glimpse of movement in the shadow of the cliff. She turned in slow motion. If a wild animal charged her, she had her cast iron pan as a defense. Not enough protection from a hungry mountain lion or bear. She hefted the pan anyway into a fighting position. Her heart hammered hard against her ribs. The shadowed form grew larger.

With a sigh, and a smile, Summer Sky recognized her mother's missing horse as the ominous shadow came closer.

"It's just Sunshine looking for breakfast." Summer Sky laughed at her own fear, and the horse looked up then back down as she dug for more grass in the snow. Wind jostled her again, as if laughing at her, then he headed toward his companion, curious about what she may have found.

Summer Sky spotted a fresh patch of snow and scooped a panful, carried it back and set it on the fire. Not finding enough grass, both horses ambled over by the fire where they checked her pan for oatcakes.

"That's my breakfast, get your nose out of there." Summer Sky chastised Wind as she chuckled and shoved him away. Then, the memory of why they trekked through the wilderness alone rushed in. Burying her mother flooded back with a slap, sobering her mood. Somehow, guilt swarmed her for finding joy in the simple things her animals had done. Joy in forgetting. Forgetting her loss and pain seemed easier once she had left the village. Sighing and taking several breaths, she stirred her bubbling pan of corn meal and dried huckleberries.

Summer Sky sat cross legged on her sleeping mat with her breakfast and set it on Wind's wool saddle pad, taking her first bite. She watched the horses searching for grass and wondered which direction she should go. The horses needed a gradual grade, making it easier with the two travois. If only she had a map or the experience the hunters had of this region.

As she finished her meal, a plan formed. She scanned the hills above her shelter. Summer Sky swiped snow around in her pan, cleaning it as best she could without water, and packed it. Then she put the travois back together for yet another exhausting day, moving her village of three up the snowy hills toward her isolated future.

When she finished harnessing the horses, she reached into the pouch she had slung over one shoulder and pulled out two oatcakes. She fed her helpers, while gratitude filled her for their steadfast loyalty. Summer Sky knew she'd need them every step of the way. While Wind nuzzled her palm for every crumb of oatcake, Summer Sky touched her forehead against his, giving God her gratitude and thanks for sustaining them.

Recalling the morning scare, Summer Sky slung her bow and quiver of arrows onto her back, prepared for trouble or even a chance of fresh meat. Moving along the base of the cliff, around the edge of the meadow, she reached a stand of cotton wood.

Summer Sky inspected the damp, sweet fragrant buds of the tree. The time for the harvest had passed, the bud tight with frost, but she picked one off a branch anyway and kept it in her palm. She rubbed the warmed bud, covered her face, and inhaled the strong, sweet woodsy scent. The fragrance brought memories of when she and her mother had gathered and prepared cottonwood bud tea for colds and flu symptoms.

She smiled as her mind raced back to a happy time gathering with her mother. Her fingers stained brown and sticky with resin, Summer Sky had gotten them stuck in her hair and her mother had to help untangle the mess. She dropped the bud onto the snow and wiped her hands on her coat. The banks of the Pend Oreille River, near her village, had a plentiful supply of Cottonwoods.

A deep sigh escaped her lips. She wondered what she

would find growing around her new home. As soon as she had chosen a place she would explore for plants, as well as she could in winter. She would gather some cottonwood twigs in the spring if she could find some. Once the buds had dried on the twigs, she and her mother had stored them in jars, preserving their medicinal strength. The twigs made tea for inflammation and pain relief which may come in handy should she hurt herself.

Wind followed behind her, and Sunshine trailed after Wind. Summer Sky trudged along leading the way through the wide cottonwoods, watching, and contemplating her surroundings. She stopped, orienting herself with the terrain and the level of the sun. A hint of frustration settled in her gut. Wandering around in circles in the woods would ruin her quest for independence. She guessed their trek had taken them northeast since the sun warmed her right cheek.

As the cottonwoods disappeared, replaced with grand fir, western hemlock, and tamarack, the going got much trickier. She shortened the travois a bit. Summer Sky picked her way through the area searching for the widest paths, which slowed them down. The slower pace, however, conserved energy and gave Summer Sky time to choose their direction with careful thought.

After hours, pushing toward early afternoon, their uphill progress became evident when they broke out of the trees onto a bench between two mountains. Far below she could see the river. Summer Sky stopped for a break. Her stomach growled when she opened her food bag for a cold patty of cornmeal and huckleberries she had made from her breakfast.

"Wind, do you want some of this?" She broke the patty in half and fed Wind as she pulled the harness from his back, lowering the travois. The snow had deepened as they had climbed higher up the mountainside. She must leave her snowshoes on or sink.

Summer Sky unharnessed Sunshine as well, giving her the other half of the corn patty.

"Good girl, thank you for helping me, my friend." Summer Sky hugged her around the neck then released her.

By the legs of the horses, she gauged the powder would reach her thighs should she take her snowshoes off. She scouted the clearing for a stump or downed tree to enjoy her break with the other cornmeal cake and a strip of venison jerky, watching the horses roll and play in the deep snow.

Looking across the valley along the river, Summer Sky tried to discern her location by the smoke she could see curling in the far distance. She blew out a frustrated breath. Before the sickness she would have used the smoke from her village to gauge where she stood. Still, she wondered about the chimneys she could see in the far distance. She couldn't recall the name of the town where her father had had his dairy farm.

Trepidation welled up inside her, she counted at least a dozen structures using wood for heat. A schoolhouse and even a store and a church. Summer Sky's mother had told her about a church they had attended, another part of their tragic love story.

"Oh, papa, if only I had you here with me right now." Summer Sky shouldn't dwell on the what if or despair might overwhelm her, stealing her resolve to push on.

"Hardship makes one stronger." She said the words aloud but heard her mother's voice in her head. She sighed, missing her mother, a physical pressure in her chest. Her future seemed dark and lonely, as if the light had faded a few feet in front of her.

"I guess that's why it's called blind faith, not knowing what the future will bring. Today has enough trouble, tomorrow will take care of itself." Summer Sky said, quoting her mother's wise words from the bible.

With that in mind, Summer Sky whistled for her faithful friends. They continued toward that future, further away from the view of the Pend' Oreille River, where a lifetime of memories had threatened to drown her. She headed north along the saddle between the two mountains and traveled the ridgeline, keeping the view of the river for as long as she could.

CHAPTER TWELVE

Summer Sky followed the ridgeline over two more mountains and back down. The crest had fewer trees, less bunched up. She and the horses pushed their way up the third mountainside of the day. She must find her campsite for the night. As soon as that thought faded, a cliff came into view that blocked her path.

Frustrated by the delay, she took a calculated look around. On her right, an old tree stuck out of the middle of a flat spot in the snow. The bark had long since sluffed off which left just the sun-bleached wood of its trunk and branches.

"Hmm, I think that might be a lake." She spoke to Wind as she pointed it out to him. The horse chuffed as if he agreed. She trekked in the direction where she assumed the lake would have an inlet. Not ten feet away she could hear the bubbling and splashing of the creek draining into the frozen pond.

Summer Sky scanned the area. It had possibilities. She had few necessities. Water, wood, food, shelter. The little valley had it all. Most of the winter winds came from the west and the north. A rock wall north of her protected the valley from the harshest of winds. The west had a hillside of timber and she noticed bushes on the edge of the clearing with pinkish red leaves poking out of the snow which resembled huckleberry bushes. She imagined sunset in the little valley happening fast this time of the year.

The sun filtered through the trees and angled through a clearing on the ridge above her. It spread its golden twilight rays on the cliff, bathing it in pink, red and lavender shades. It took her breath away. She looked toward the east and estimated where the sun would rise. Since she loved watching the sunrise, her excitement mounted as she pulled the travois poles out of the harness over Wind's back and lowered it. She then released Sunshine from her burden, and the two wandered through the deep snow toward the inlet for a drink.

Summer Sky followed, pulling her empty water pouch from her coat. The horses finished their drink and moved on, hunting for their dinner of dried grass. She bent low, reaching the trickle of water flowing over a rock and set the mouth of her bag underneath.

The spring made fetching water so much easier than melting snow in her cooking pan. She took a long drink and relished the freshness as it slid down her parched throat. How long had they traveled? Two, maybe three days? The cadence of life in the forest seemed simpler. She didn't care about time, she only cared about the change of seasons and how long until spring. For this reason, she decided she must keep track.

Coming up from the stream she noticed how far the sun had set. Setting up her tipi could wait. She lacked shelter for one more night, but it didn't bother her. She had found her new home.

Summer Sky slid the pile of sleeping furs off the travois onto a flat spot in the middle of the clearing, grabbed two strips of jerky, then snuggled in for the night. She pulled her fur-lined hood over her head and laid with her face toward the sky, thinking about her mother and father together in heaven.

She imagined joy filling her father's face as Water Lily ran to him. The laughter and hugs they shared. Did her father swing her mother around in a tight embrace while the angels and Jesus danced with them? Longing for her parents flooded her senses as the jerky tasted like dirt in her mouth. She choked on the dry meat as it stuck itself against the lump in her throat.

"Mama, Papa... if only you could come for me. Do you even care that your little girl is all alone?" Summer Sky swallowed the wad of jerky, along with the shame she struggled with for wanting to give up and join her parents.

The overwhelming thoughts drained from her as she studied the star dappled sky. Peace washed over her, and she somehow understood that God had a plan for her life. With a sigh, Summer Sky relaxed into the sleeping firs.

It didn't matter that she ate cold food and drank icy water. The sky through the night delighted her. She watched fluffy clouds scuttle past and hide the stars, then they popped out even brighter on the other side. Shooting stars filled the sky.

"Thank you, God, for the beautiful sky tonight. Thank you for showing me you're still with me." Delighted by the lights in the sky, she watched for hours imagining herself with her parents admiring the show together.

CHAPTER THIRTEEN

A red sky in the east greeted Summer Sky as she peeked out of her sleeping furs. She had grown up hearing the old saying regarding a red sunrise, warning the people of a coming storm. It proved as accurate as all the other sayings. She blinked sleep out of her eyes and searched her surroundings for signs of impending doom. Studying the blue sky eased her fear, the calm and sunny day proved she had some time. A gentle breeze from the west gave her comfort, the "red sky" hadn't pushed toward her location. Not yet.

Now, where should I place my village of one? No, make that three. Summer Sky mused while she scanned the expanse of white. A village of three, at least while her horse friends stayed with her.

Summer Sky pushed the covers off and shivered. She missed the warmth of her cocoon of furs. Her breath shrouded her head with clouds of sunrise hued vapor. The weather may prove unpredictable, she must focus on setting up her camp.

With a roof over her head in mind, Summer Sky explored the area. She tromped through the knee-high fluffy snow, searching for the flattest spot. She'd use the treed hillside on the west of her as a wind break. But not too close, avoiding the dangers from wild animals. Even a tall fir tree could topple onto her tipi with the weight of heavy snow. If something should charge her from the forest, she'd have time to defend herself.

She trekked up the hill toward the northern cliff and assessed the winds. She calculated the distance between her camp and the stream for convenience. Looking east she had a clear view of the sunrise over the layers of misty mountains that faded into grey green on the horizon. She loved the beauty of her new home.

She realized, as she gazed toward the east, that she stood on the perfect spot. She whistled for Wind and Sunshine and turned in the direction of her piled up belongings near the stream.

Summer Sky harnessed the horses and attached the travois, hopefully, for the last time. Despite the short distance, their help made it so much easier. Once she reached the flat space she had chosen and unloaded, Wind bumped her toward the travois.

"Did I confuse you, boy? Good news, my friend, this is our home now." Summer Sky wrapped her arms around Wind, leaning against his warm winter fur.

"Home." She pushed away with renewed stamina.

She untied the poles for her tipi from the travois and laid them out in the snow the way her mother had taught her. She stared at the formation and a niggling of doubt crept in. She had never put the tipi up by herself. Again, she needed help from her friends. She tied the top of the poles together with two long ropes, then tied them onto the horses' harnesses. With Wind on her left and Sunshine on her right, she commanded them, hoping they'd listen.

"Hup, hup," she uttered, as she pulled the middle pole between them. They both turned their heads and gave her a look which conveyed their confusion. With a heavy sigh, she pulled on Wind's harness, and he stepped forward, repeated the command, then did the same with Sunshine.

She joined them again holding one of the tall pine posts and tugged hard.

"Hup, hup," and the horses pulled. The tipi poles lifted. The plan worked.

"Ho, steady." They held the tipi in place as she righted each pole in their spots, keeping them upright once she had released the horses.

Rolling out the shell of her tipi, she set the door toward the rising sun and situated the poles a bit more. She walked around the laid-out wall, wondering how the adults had erected the tipis. She had never watched someone set one up alone.

Summer Sky threaded a rope into the smoke hole flap and threw it over the spikes at the top. She prayed it landed in the precise spot. After the sixth attempt, she groaned. Her mother had the experience she lacked. She racked her brain going over the steps her mother had taken, praying she'd figure it out.

"Please, God. I need help."

As if He'd already answered, a thought struck her. With renewed hope, she tied the rope from the smoke hole flap onto the pole that controlled the opening and guided it over the tipi as if she had done it many times.

Relief flooded Summer Sky. With the Lord's help she finished the most important part of the process. She lowered the pole and untied the rope then pulled until her muscles shook. She sat down with a huff. The process had always been a group effort. They had all helped each other. Her aunt and uncle set up theirs with their son's help, then they'd help she and her mother.

Summer Sky didn't have the luxury of family and friends. She wallowed in her own limitations until the beauty of her new home distracted her. At the downhill side of the flat ice-covered lake, she saw movement. Over the white lump of sticks and logs at the outlet of the lake, a dark little head popped up and watched her. Its small round face tilted as if asking "What are you doing here?"

A smile spread across Summer Sky's face as she watched the beaver hide then show its face in another place on the pile. She owed the little critter thanks for the small lake so near her home. What a wonderful place. Sharing the view with her mother would fill her heart with gladness. Desperate loneliness niggled at her. Anxiety swelled in her chest, and she took several deep breaths. Her mind flooded with all the things that might go wrong.

After the sixth or seventh long, lung-filling breath, she realized she must make the shell lighter at the top. She walked around the long outer layer of her tipi. She looked at the tie straps at intervals that matched the poles, and a possible solution arose.

First, Summer Sky dragged the right bottom corner of the cover in place where she wanted the doorway and tied the straps. She worked her way around, securing the wall onto each corresponding support. She adjusted the poles as she went, ending at the last one on the other side of the door opening. She repeated the pattern, circling around the opposite direction. She had worked the cover as high as she could over her head, then tried pulling the rope again. Still too heavy. She worried the rope might tear the smoke hole flap, rendering it useless.

She'd finished only half of the tipi. Her muscles screamed at her for a break. Heat crept over her face and tears blurred her vision. She laid the heels of her hands over her eyes and pushed them away. Anger welled up inside her. Anger at herself for being too weak on her own. Anger at her decision about living alone and not as her mother had said. Staying with her uncle may have been the easier choice. Anger seemed more manageable, instead of the overwhelming fear and doubts she faced daily.

"Why can't I figure this out?" She growled as she stomped around the wrinkled and collapsing cover. It looked pathetic draped over the poles. She noticed the time; the sun had passed the noon position. Her stomach growled as sweat trickled down her back. Rolling her eyes, she huffed out a heavy sigh that shrouded her head in moisture and again chided herself for not drinking and eating.

Sitting on a pile of her belongings, she took another break visualizing her future outdoor firepit as she nibbled on a dry strip of jerky. A small pit would work for her. She believed she'd seen the materials she needed at the rock wall north of her. Maybe doing something else might bring her clarity when she returned.

Summer Sky grabbed the skin sled, her food bag, her water pouch, and her bow and quiver of arrows. She strapped everything over her shoulders and tied on her snowshoes. As she wandered up the hill, her excitement grew as more beauty met her. The untouched winter scene took her breath away.

Her thoughts on the firepit, she headed north. As she passed a stand of small fir trees, she noticed a flat spot halfway up the cliff that angled toward the top. With further exploration, she might find caves on that ledge. Shaking her head, she tabled that thought for later. The camp must take precedence for at least the next few days.

As she neared the bottom of the cliff, a blast of wind plunged down her neck. She scanned the sky, as it filled with dark clouds. Time for exploring had run out. She needed shelter, and soon.

Racing down the hillside as fast as her snowshoes allowed, she whistled for Wind and Sunshine. With the fast-approaching storm, she had no choice. She must chance ripping the smoke hole flap. Summer Sky trusted that if she put the pole through the hole on the other side, then she might guide it while Wind pulled? She must try.

She attached the rope onto the smoke hole and then around Wind's chest, grabbing his lead rope. She could stop him with the lead in case the task got out of control. Summer Sky positioned herself on the other side of the tipi, holding the long pole that controlled the smoke flap. Next, she shoved the pole in with the rope and lifted it as high as she could.

"Are you ready?" She asked Wind and the horse neighed his answer.

"Ok, Lord, the storm is almost upon us, but you control the weather. I am your child, please calm the storm within me, as well as the one in the sky." Peace flooded over her.

"Hup, hup" she called out, and the cover lifted. She kept the lead tight, instructing Wind with slow and small movements. Pushing the smoke hole pole up higher as the cover lifted into place.

"Ho, boy. Excellent work, my friend."

She inhaled, filling her lungs. She'd forgotten to breathe

through that entire process. With the smoke hole flap in place, she adjusted the outer layer of her home. Then she grabbed the bag of bone pins to secure the edges together. She stood in the middle of her new doorway and secured the first pin at the top of the door.

Once she'd attached three pins, she climbed onto the cover. Using the pins like rungs on a ladder, she fastened the rest. While at the top of her tipi, she secured the smoke hole cover and untied the rope from the flap. Bitter wind whipped loosened whisps of hair into her eyes and snowflakes filtered down her back. She had no time left. The storm had arrived.

Sliding down the tipi, she hit the ground and ran for the mound of household belongings. Summer Sky whistled for the horses while she dragged everything inside. She made one last trip and called again. No horses. They must have scurried into the woods for shelter.

Instead of worrying, she searched for the new door flap she had taken from Merri's tipi. She had wrapped it in the inner wall lining. Anxious about the storm she couldn't decide what she must do next. The walls, the poles, the door, all seemed necessary for protection from the storm. A blast of wind almost toppled the tipi over. She dove for the side the wind lifted and caught it in time. The priority had made itself known. First, she pushed the poles as far outward as the shell allowed and secured them with stakes.

After an hour of fighting with the wind, her arms and back ached. She secured the last few poles as the wind shoved against the sides. The storm threatened the work she and the horses had done. Determined, she hammered the last stake in and yanked the door flap out of the pile.

Breathing hard, with an exhausted grip she wrestled with the flap as the wind almost yanked it from her. First one tie, then the next, she focused on the task in front of her.

Before she slipped the toggle into its holes that closed the door flap, wind slapped her face with icy flakes. Falling on her knees, gratitude washed through her with a sigh as tears of relief dripped off her chin. The stress of the storm hit her, and she collapsed against the door. The wind screamed through the trees and slammed the tiny tipi as if it were a physical entity. Fear swelled in Summer Sky and displaced her momentary relief.

"Mama, please help me. I know you can't, but I need you so much." She screamed out for her mother in her exhaustion, in her fear and uncertainty something bad might happen. With every gust she cried out her fear. The wind blasted and the tipi shuddered.

"God help me." Summer Sky shouted over the roar of the wind which found its way inside her shelter. Yes, something bad could very well happen tonight. The realization of freezing in the wind chill if her tipi fell apart seemed a great possibility as she clung to the wall the wind shoved against the most. But then a thought slipped into her mind. If it did, then she would wake with her parents and her King.

The awareness of her faith filled her. No matter what happened, Summer Sky depended only on God for her welfare. Comfort settled the frantic beat of her heart. Then, she heard a howl, and her heartbeat tripled its cadence. She heard it again, closer. Listening for the answering howls that meant more than one, the air remained silent.

She held her breath and waited, listening until her lungs demanded air. Still nothing. As she caught her breath, her mind raced with a list of howling animals and resigned herself with the only possibility.

Wolf.

Its voice sounded too deep for a coyote or fox. She respected the wild animals which coexisted in the wilderness with humans. She'd invaded his territory, not the other way around. She worried about the horses. They hadn't returned and they may not until the storm blew itself out.

She stood with effort. Her stomach growled. She had forgotten about food, again. She looked around at the scattered piles of her belongings and sighed. She must do better.

CHAPTER FOURTEEN

Sunlight filtered through the cracks around the smoke hole flap and the door ties. Her heart filled with gladness; the storm had passed. She lay under her warm furs and planned the day.

"The horses." She sat up with a start. She must check on the horses.

A moment later, she heard a pushing and chuffing at the door flap.

"Good morning." Summer Sky sang out as she stood, taking her sleeping fur with her. When she pulled the toggle out of the door, Wind stuck his head in and nudged her. She scratched him behind his ear then laid her forehead against his. Joy that her friends had weathered the storm flooded over her. They didn't seem any worse off because of it. With a sigh, she wrapped her arms around Wind, resting against him with her eyes closed.

Exhaustion weakened her, and she leaned against her horse's warm neck. The storm had kept Summer Sky awake holding down tipi poles through the night. Her stomach growled, and Wind's head shot up, he seemed surprised by the sound emanating from her middle.

"It's ok boy. I'm just hungry. I imagine you and Sunshine are too, by the looks of the amount of snow that piled up last night." Summer Sky said as she squinted.

The sun glared off the bright white snow outside, blinding, and cold. She shivered even with the warm fur wrapped around her.

Later that day she'd gather rocks for her fire pits, both

inside and outside. Wind could carry the load, but she'd used the poles setting up her tipi. Perhaps, she could build a drag from the hair-covered hide she had used in the past.

But first, another cold breakfast.

"In or out, my friend," Summer Sky said, while chucking Wind under the chin. She pulled back the door flap and stepped aside, allowing room for him to enter but Wind backed up and turned away. Assuming he'd gone after his breakfast, she thought it a clever idea.

Glancing around the messy interior of her home, she frowned at the haphazard piles in the middle of the space. With the surprise storm, she hadn't organized any of it. She noticed the wall cover out of the corner of her eye, then she stopped herself.

"First things first. Breakfast, then work." Summer Sky reminded herself. Getting caught up in all the work, before she'd consider the place home, proved hard to ignore. However, neglecting her body's needs could cause greater harm than the elements. She could get weak and sick.

Who would take care of me?

Shaking her head, Summer Sky sighed.

She searched through the piles of belongings for her food, lost somewhere under all the baskets and skins and pans and pouches. With a frustrated huff and another growl of her tummy, she fished through the mess. She found her water pouch and food bag at the bottom.

Chewing on a jerky strip, she organized her home. Out of habit, her thoughts centered on how her mother had organized things. Did she want it to look the same and remind her of her mother every time she entered the tipi? As if she would see her mother at any moment come through the door? No, she must step through the grief and fold her mother's memory away in the past or she may not survive.

Summer Sky stood in the center of the room and visualized where things should go. Her mother had kept the medicinal shelves and workbench in the back, but Summer Sky opted for a spot with more light near the door. Besides, she would work plants only for herself and not an entire village, at least for a while. Maybe once she grew up, she could study under another healer. She lacked the confidence to take on so much responsibility. Taking care of herself overwhelmed her enough.

With the workbench and shelves on the west side of the room, her sleeping pallet must go in the back. With the fire between her and the door, she'd have more security. Would she need so many shelves, or could she use the wood for a wall behind her bed? A barrier from the cold that seeped through the skins of the tipi seemed possible. And, on the east side, she'd set up her kitchen supplies and firewood storage area.

Now that she had a plan, she pulled another strip of jerky from her pouch. She peeked inside. Her supply of meat needed replenished, and soon. She chewed, savoring the salty, smoky flavor as she scraped away the snow from her new floor using her shovel and a pail. She worked in sections and moved her belongings as she went. Every time she filled the pail, she took it outside. She dumped it around the edges of her tipi and packed it down. Snow worked as a great insulator; it kept the drafts from finding their way under the shell.

A few hours later, around mid-morning, she had her floor cleared of snow. It pleased her, the dirt under the grass and snow had a good amount of clay and very few rocks. It made for a nice smooth floor; she flattened it with little effort. Her mother had taught her to fill a glass jar half full of water. Then when she laid it on its side, she could see if the floor slanted.

After Summer Sky leveled the ground, she stomped it down with her feet for several turns until sweat dampened her forehead. It took enormous effort. When she'd finished, she worked on tethering the inner wall in place. She needed the wood crate. Jars and baskets of dried plants and tinctures her mother had made, filled the crate. Dragging it over toward the building supplies for her shelves she set aside each parcel.

The inner lining of her tipi seemed an arduous task by herself. She and her mother had slumped down against each other, taking a break with an oat cake and tea. The bittersweet memory swam through her mind with every secure tie. She missed their laughter and comradery. Summer Sky's mother had been her best friend, her only friend. A stab of pain pierced through her chest, crushing. She dropped to her knees.

"Lord, I know you must have saved me for a reason. I am grateful, but I am also so very alone. I know I chose this, but I didn't see any other way." Summer Sky whispered a prayer, confident God heard her. The familiar peace filled the empty space in her heart, and she could breathe again.

She took several breaths, slow in and slow out. She dragged herself off the packed dirt floor. She must not give into despair. Her lack of motivation hammered at her resolve, but at least she had made progress.

"How would my mother counsel me if I were her patient?" She spoke aloud, bolstering her strength. A memory popped into her mind of her mother with a patient who had struggled with the loss of a baby.

"Do the next thing." Summer Sky mimicked her mother. Doing the next thing seemed like her mother's prescription for every sadness.

Water Lily had told Summer Sky. "It is easier to give in and give up, but if one looks at what is next, not the big, sad picture, small chunks of life seemed less daunting." At least she still had her mother's advice, if only in her head.

"Do the next pole." She repeated as she made her way around the room. She collapsed onto her sleeping fur. Lying on her back she studied the light that angled through the smoke hole. She'd worked all morning, and she wanted to have the hearth finished by sunset. She'd stay warmer than she had the night before.

Groaning while pulling herself to her feet, she sorted through the pile of furs and skins, finding the hair sled she needed. Summer Sky grabbed a rope and draped her sled over her shoulder, then left the tipi. Scanning the sky and the horizon for any signs of weather for another surprise storm, she whistled for Wind and Sunshine.

The horses grazed at the far end of the lake. Summer Sky whistled again as she strapped on her snowshoes. Then, heading uphill toward the cliff, she hoped she'd find round rocks for building her hearth.

Wind came up beside her and chuffed a greeting. Sunshine trailed behind in his footsteps conserving energy by following his path of broken snow. Summer Sky had noticed all wildlife had the same habit. Using that knowledge, she'd replenish her meat, placing her wire traps along the trails in the snow she found.

Once she had built her hearth, she would set traps out and check them in the morning. Lord willing, she would have fresh meat tomorrow. For tonight she would cook a stew with the remaining dried strips of venison she had left in her pouch. A warm meal might motivate her despite her over-tired muscles.

They reached the cliff. A wide vein of gravel and larger rocks made pulling it apart easy. Taking a sharp rock from the wall, she chipped away at a promising area and gathered long, flat rocks onto her hair sled. She could build up the side toward the door a bit higher, keeping the drafts from affecting her fire. The higher wall would direct the heat into the sleeping area throughout the night as well. Sunshine trailed them as they returned with the first load. If she had another fur, she'd load up both horses and have enough rock for two fire pits.

On the next trip, she used Sunshine, while Wind trailed, keeping them company. Summer Sky dumped the rocks they had gathered into a pile and started building her hearth. First, she dug a trough in an oval shape. One side would hold the fire and on the other side, she'd heap coals, making a place for baking once she had unpacked her cast iron oven. As she worked, her mouth watered, thinking of the bread she would bake.

Next, she needed rocks. She carried them one at a time and selected them from the pile hoping they would fit together like a ring of puzzle pieces. She gathered a pile of the rejected ones, hoping they'd work for the next layer.

The project took most of the day, and she kept an eye on the daylight streaming through the smoke hole. She could tell time by the line of shadow and sunlight following the poles. A watch, like the one the chief had, showed the exact time, but her method worked for what she needed. She kept track of how long until sunset, wanting a blazing fire before dark.

CHAPTER FIFTEEN

As Summer Sky set the last brick-like rock on her fire pit inside her tipi, her stomach growled.

"Mama, you would love this fireplace. It's better than anything we have had except maybe the one you told me about in your little farmhouse by the lake you and Papa had." Her mind wandered through memories of her mother as she grabbed a corncake from her food pouch and devoured it down with water.

She raised her head and gauged the sun's position, an hour or less until sunset. She still needed a load of wood for her first fire. Grabbing her fur sled and her saw from the toolbox, she headed into the stand of trees toward the west.

Her mother had taught her the lower limbs of fir trees die off as a tree grows. The branches stayed dry under the close-fitting needles that sheltered the underside. When harvesting, cutting three fingers from the trunk protected the tree from insects.

God had blessed her with a beautiful area. As she cut branches and laid them on her fur, she inhaled the fresh smell from her growing wood pile. She watched as the cliff exploded with a brilliant array of sunset colors.

"Am I home, Lord? I sure hope so." Contentment floated out of her on a sigh and a smile. Summer Sky stepped out from under the tree for a moment, relishing the scene as the colors changed in rapid succession. She must hurry.

She foraged under the trees for dried leaves and needles and cones, filling out her stockpile of materials. She dumped the debris into the middle of the branches piled on the fur, finishing her first load.

She dragged the fur right through the door and toward the outer edge, designated as her wood storage area. Summer Sky had plenty of time after the sun went down for organizing. She took a handful of fluffy dry leaves and needles and placed it in the middle of her new fireplace. Then, broke off small twigs covered in lichen, stacking them around the tinder. She dumped the rest against the wall and headed back out for more.

She continued until dark, making navigating the forest impossible. After all the trips dragging the fur sled, she'd packed down a nice trail in the snow, making her trek easier. The last trip she left her snowshoes in the tipi.

As the dim rays of sunlight left the cliff above her, Summer Sky's eyes scanned her new home for the horses, but she didn't see them. Since horses often bedded down before sunset, she wouldn't worry. She said a prayer for safe keeping for herself and her friends and secured the door flap for the night.

Complete darkness enclosed her in the tipi. She hadn't planned that well. Sensing her way through the dark with her foot, she inched toward the firepit, avoiding stubbing her toe. Then, she scrounged around for her fire-starting kit but couldn't find it. On all fours, she searched for anything resembling her food bag.

"Got it," she whispered out loud as she pulled the bag out from under a haphazard pile of random items. "The last time I noticed, my fire kit was somewhere near the food bag."

She sighed in relief when she found it covered by the fur sled. She had slid it inside and hadn't unloaded it yet. Her hunger reared up, voracious. Crawling, she gathered what she needed and felt around for the leaves she'd dumped in the firepit. She added the cattail fluff from the bag and positioned her flint.

Seven strikes which blinded her for a few seconds each time. The dark invaded the space once the spark died. The flares of light, followed by pitch darkness kept her from finding the sweet spot on the flint where she could get the best spark. The cattail fluff caught fire. The leaves slowed the flame from consuming the fluff too fast. She added moss, more twigs, and bark from the branches she'd harvested. Summer Sky had the first fire in her new hearth and home.

She tended the fire until it had a good blaze going, ensuring it wouldn't go out, then grabbed her pan and headed outside to fetch water at the stream for tea. As she stood with her full pan and turned back toward the tipi, the bushes rustled near where she had cut the firewood. She froze. If a predator lurked nearby, she'd stand her ground. She moved slow, making herself look as tall as possible while still holding her pan in front of her. She listened, hearing nothing more and walked into her tipi, forcing away the thought of a wild animal hiding somewhere in the dark, just out of sight.

She closed herself in for the night, secure with the new door flap, and threw more wood on the fire. The hearth bounced glorious light throughout her home. Water droplets sizzled on the bottom of her pan as she set it near her new fire. Then, she placed two strips of dried venison in her skillet, and sprinkled flour over them. She still hadn't found the jar of fat; it would have given her stew more flavor. She tipped her pan and poured a little water into the skillet. It spat and sizzled and danced across the hot cast iron, filling the air with savory steam.

Hunger gnawed at her gut; she hadn't eaten since breakfast. She had oats and ground corn in her food bag, she chose corn and sprinkled a good portion of the cornmeal across the top of the meat and water. Somewhere, she had a bag of potatoes and some dried vegetables. She'd worry about locating them later, but for tonight she'd have warm food and a warm bed, and light.

Exhaustion dragged at her movements, yet the list of tasks needing her attention seemed daunting. She chose the ones which took less effort and would make the night easier. She sat cross-legged in front of her wood pile, breaking branches the right length and stacking them: Kindling, small finger, and thumb. Twig fires burned fast and needed tending more often through the night. Tomorrow she'd get larger pieces of wood, which meant chopping down a tree.

As she sorted and stacked, she looked for a long, straight branch, bigger than her thumb in thickness for her counting stick. She found one near the bottom of her pile and stood it beside her, measuring its height. It reached a bit over her head and when she leaned on it, it held her weight. She had an idea. Summer Sky searched for the deer-skin pouch which stored her carving knife, along with other knives and small tools.

"Such a mess, I can't find anything. Tomorrow I must build the workbench and shelves."

Her voice sounded raspy from lack of use as she growled out her frustration at the mess. She shoved boxes and bags around in her search and found the tool pouch tucked in a crate of jars filled with dried herbs and tinctures.

Sitting in front of the fire on a cattail weaved mat, she stripped the bark off her counting stick, stuffing the shavings into an empty basket. After it dries, she'd grind it down in case she should come down with a cold. For protection, she whittled the top end into a sharp point. She'd use it for multiple purposes. She would decorate it as the winter progressed and come spring, take it with her as a walking stick as well.

She had decided the first notch on her stick should mark the first day of her journey. Despite her aloneness, she counted how many days had passed, including the day she had said her good-byes. She also tracked whether she had missed Christmas.

Winter had played tricks on her in the past and misnumber the days. Her mother had taught her the importance of planning when spring would bring fresh greens and new grass for the horses. But she had months of winter, and plenty of busy work until the days grew longer.

Thinking back as she carved the notches, she counted. The day she dug Yellow Dock roots, Christmas had been a month away. A week later, the coughing person asked her mother for help. Could she have missed it? She couldn't imagine Christmas without her mother. Regardless of whether she had missed Christmas, she would celebrate her Savior's birth anyway.

It didn't matter which day, but that she observed His

birth. Summer Sky celebrated Jesus every day in some way. He had become her sole companion, aside from her horses. If only He could hold her.

Her eyes clouded, and she couldn't see her carvings. She sniffled, stifling the tears that threatened, and changed her train of thought. Once she had finished setting up her home and had her traps out, she planned on celebrating Christmas with her first kill.

CHAPTER SIXTEEN

Summer Sky stoked the fire through the night which took most of her woodpile. In the morning, she poured hot water from her kettle into her cooking pan. The radiant heat off the hearthstones had kept the kettle warm. Her new home filled her with happiness, she thanked God again for his blessings as she placed her hands on the flat rocks, warming her fingers.

Then, the long days and nights sleeping against the communal firepit, as she and her mother fought for the lives of the people, gripped her heart, and brought the sadness back. Her chest constricted in pain for her mother. She wished she could share this beautiful, secluded world she had found. She missed her mother's love to the point of physical pain.

Slumping down in front of the fire with a sigh, she set the pan of water over the coals, making hot tea and cornmeal cereal. Dried huckleberries would taste wonderful in her cereal. Even though she had a limited supply in her stockpile of dried berries, she couldn't pass them up. She reached into her food bag grabbing the tiny, purple, dried temptations and sprinkled them into her cereal then added the last of her thumb-sized sticks on the fire and boiled tea water. She picked up her walking stick, counting another day.

Summer Sky dressed in her warm fur leggings and parka as her cereal bubbled in the skillet nestled in the hot coals. She finished her breakfast, laid the door flap over the outside wall, and watched the sun peak through the trees on the other side of the pond sipping her tea as it warmed her hands. The serenity of her surroundings enveloped her, and she closed her eyes, the sun warming her face.

"Mama, you would have loved it here."

Summer Sky willed herself to imagine her mother standing beside her. She closed her eyes and wrapped her own arms around her as she hugged herself. The image seemed so vivid she refused to open her eyes and pulled from her memory the scent of lavender and lemongrass her mother had added to her soap when she made it every fall. The scent wafted around her and warmed her soul yet tightened her chest with a heavy longing for her mother's comfort. The tightness swelled up her throat and as hard as she tried swallowing it back down, she couldn't stop the flood overflowing her eyelids.

Summer Sky didn't fight it this time, grieving her mother for the first time since her death. No storm. No pressure. This morning, she allowed herself the luxury of emotion, and she wallowed in it. She slid onto her knees, stared out the door, and sobbed. Holding her warm mug of tea against her cold cheek, she wanted her mother's hand there, a warm cup could never supply the solace of her mother's presence.

"I miss you so much," Summer Sky whispered like a prayer. She pulled on the sleeves of her parka as if the pressure might help her recover from such a great loss. As if the pressure made her less lonely.

"Lord, thank you for taking care of me. I know you are with me. I still want my mother though." With her arms around herself, she rocked. Her tears dripped off her chin unchecked as she raised her face toward heaven as an agonized groan slipped past her lips.

"Thank you, Lord, for your comfort." As soon as the words left her lips her restricted lungs filled with crisp morning air and calm flooded through her with her exhale, into every part of her.

With a restorative peace in her heart, she surveyed her messy home. Resolve replaced her grief, time to put what she can control into place.

Leaving the door flap open and with sun streaming through the smoke hole, daylight eased her efforts. She shoved the crates and bags away from the area she had designated as her workspace, then dragged the heavy ten-inch-wide boards where she wanted them. She sorted the poles they rested on and assembled a frame. Rummaging through a crate, she found her mallet and the pegs that secured the frame together. A great start on organizing her life.

* * *

With a trickle of sweat tickling its way down her back, Summer Sky rested in front of the fire and admired her work. She relished her plan for organizing everything. She had found her root vegetables at the bottom of the tool crate. Putting her kettle on the coals, she steeped some bee balm and wild rosehip tea.

Do the next thing. Her mother's voice whispered from the past. As she found a place for everything and put everything in its place, it gave her a sense of pride, pleasure and relief all rolled up in a giant package of accomplishment.

Her next thing, gathering wood larger than her thumb so it burned longer than the sticks she had used in her fire the night before. She'd need the horse's help hauling the wood.

She rummaged in her food pouch for an oat cake or two so that she could keep working. She had hung it on a peg near her storage shelves. She and her mother had added pegs on the tipi poles at convenient heights for clothing and various bags and utensils; her fire starter pouch hung near the wood pile, coats at the door, and her food pouch where she'd stacked the cooking supplies on a shelf of the work bench close by the fire. Her mother had taught Summer Sky everything. They'd spent every day together since as far back as she could recall.

Chewing on a second crumbling oatcake, she unfolded the wool blankets she had dumped her and her mother's clothing in when packing. She had stuffed everything she could, rolled it up, then dragged it onto the travois. As the blanket unrolled, her mother's scent of lavender and mint filled her nostrils. Summer Sky closed her eyes, the fragrance painted a picture in her mind of her mother's face, her dark hair and laughing eyes. That amazing smile had greeted her every day of her life. The mirage seemed lifelike, as if it would make her alive again. But nothing could.

Summer Sky's knees buckled, and she buried her hands into the opening of her mother's rabbit fur lined parka then covered her face with it. She held it and imagined her mother filling the emptiness somehow.

"God, I miss my mother so much. Hold me, please." Summer Sky slid her arms through the sleeves and pulled the parka over her head.

"Hold me while I get more wood, while I set my traps and while I spend the rest of my days alone in this secluded paradise. Keep me safe if you wish it and help me keep from joining you and my family." Summer Sky stood; her mother's scent surrounded her as she slipped on the hood.

She stoked the fire and added the last of her sticks, just enough to keep the fire going until she got back with more. She slipped the quiver over her head, slid her bow over one shoulder and grabbed the hatchet she kept hanging on the doorframe. Then, she secured the door flap. Coming home with a wild animal inside her tipi, scavenging for her last bit of food, would ruin her.

Summer Sky scanned the area for her horses as she whistled. When she heard Wind neigh from the north, she searched but couldn't see him. Then, she saw movement on the snow-covered ledge halfway up the cliff. Two horses with their heads pointed downhill picked their way toward the bottom.

"You clever creatures." Summer Sky called and laughed as she realized they must have found a cave they had bedding down in. She had gotten so excited; she'd forgotten her snowshoes. She stepped off the path around her home and sunk into knee-deep powder. Cold snow flew inside the top of her moccasin where it had come loose as she worked.

Still chuckling about the brilliance of her four-legged friends, she made her way back onto the hardened path in search of her snowshoes.

Gathering enough wood for several days required dragging a log to her tipi and chopping it up instead of hauling several loads. Entering the woods west of camp, she searched the area for a dead tree still standing. A standing tree stays drier than one laying under the snow. She found one small enough for her hatchet yet big enough to make it worth her effort.

Aware of her surroundings, she searched the snow for tracks and sure enough, trails of a wolf crisscrossed the edge of the forest as if it paced along the tree line, watching.

A chill went up her spine as she scanned each tree and bush searching for it. Wind and Sunshine seemed unconcerned, so she shrugged it off and went about pushing on each trunk in search of the deadest and driest tree.

Summer Sky pulled a coil of rope from the pouch over her shoulder and wrapped it around the tree she had chosen. She hacked off big chunks of wood on one side of the trunk, and then tied the rope into a horse's harness. "Ha, Wind. Ha."

Wind pulled and the dead log cracked then fell as Summer Sky pushed it in the direction of the nearest clearing, making sure it wouldn't hit her or the horses. The trunk's width measured the length of her hatchet's head. She pulled three logs to her tipi.

Once she'd piled the logs close enough, reaching into her tipi, Summer Sky slipped her trapping bag over her head. She searched for small animal tracks in the snow. Since she had chosen this place as home, she had noticed wildlife trails surrounding her. Rabbit, squirrel, quail, grouse, pheasant, and turkey, all tracks she recognized.

As she trekked toward the outlet of the lake and the stand of timber beyond, she watched for signs in the snow. Near the edge of the trees, she spotted turkey tracks. A turkey for Christmas sounded wonderful. She could hit a turkey with an arrow, they made big targets. If she found one, since turkey's roosted high up on tree branches in the winter, making them hard to find. For the most part, she saw rabbit tracks near her home, close around the stream, and up along the bank of the frozen lake. She set a trap made from wire at the edge of the woods near the lake and worked her way further upstream.

Since she hadn't explored this far, Summer Sky nocked an arrow and kept vigilant, searching out the woods for danger. She watched her animals for agitation as well. She placed a snare trap every twenty paces along the stream, under bushes where she had found tracks. As the sun set, she placed her last trap and headed back in the alpenglow which shined off the pristine snow around her.

Using the glowing firelight filtering through the open door, Summer Sky chopped three armloads of wood and settled in for the evening. Rummaging through her food bag she brought out the last two pieces of dried venison and dropped them into her skillet. She chopped a small portion of one onion with a potato and slid the pieces in with the meat. Then she added a couple pinches of flour and hot water from her kettle, making herself a well-earned stew. Pangs of hunger swelled as the stew bubbled.

"Patience. It will taste so much better if I let it cook all the way." Summer Sky talked herself out of eating before the potatoes softened; she hadn't eaten enough as of late, considering how much work she'd done. With her camp all set up, she'd focus on food.

"Food," she mused as she stirred, then tested the softness of the meat and the potato. Getting her mind on something other than the savory smells coming from her pan, she inventoried her supplies. She had a bag of potatoes with ten or eleven of them. She stored the root vegetables in a smaller bag. It had turnips and coveted onions, a couple bunches of dried carrots and a garlic braid, enough for a few weeks, but not the entire winter.

The corn meal would last longer, and she could ration the flour.

"Not enough." She mused, placing the sack of flour on the shelf near the cornmeal with a huff. She had looked forward to making bread.

"Maybe I could bake bread once a week. But even that would only last me a few weeks. What am I going to do?"

The wind howled off the cliff and pushed against the back of her tipi. A flurry of snow filtered through the smoke hole and sizzled as it melted. A storm had snuck up on her.

Summer Sky slipped her parka over her head and stepped out the door. She adjusted the smoke hole flap so that snow couldn't get inside. The wind through the trees sounded like water rushing down a steep hillside, roaring down on her. Morning seemed a lifetime away and anxiety grew. Then, she heard the lone, sad cry of the wolf she'd worried about for the past few days. Fear erupted as she rushed back into her tent as fast as she could, fastening the door flap with trembling fingers. She dragged two heavy baskets from under the workbench, barricading the door further.

She shoved the worry settling in her stomach away. It resurfaced in an instant. What if the wolf meant her harm? At that moment, she heard something scratching at the back of her tipi. She jumped away from the sound with a yelp and crouched, her survival instinct kicking in.

Once her nerves calmed and normal breathing returned, she lit a kerosine lamp and investigated. The scratching had stopped. She stood in the middle of the circle of light, listened and weighed her options. Summer Sky glanced around the room as an idea formed.

She drew two boards from the shelving materials behind her worktable and laid out a frame on the sides of her sleeping mat. Adding another couple boards, she'd crisscrossed and nailed them together. These she used as the support for the backboard.

As she added each board, she noticed the plank wall reflected heat from the fire and blocked the drafts from the back of her tent. She ran out of shelving material and the wall reached just under her arm. The two boards she had placed on both sides of her sleeping mat supported the wall. They framed her sleeping mat at an angle. She tied them in place with baling wire wrapped around the edge of the pallet under her sleeping mat.

"One more thing," she mumbled under her breath as she pulled out six stakes from her toolbox. She pounded them into the ground with her mallet. The length of the boards they'd cut to fit along the inside wall which made a nice barrier if something found its way in behind her as she slept. It still could gain access, but not without a lot of effort and a few arrows for its trouble.

After Summer Sky finished making all the racket, while building her security wall, she stood and listened. A mouse must have tried escaping the storm in the warmth of her tipi. Whatever had made the scratching must have run off.

"I am safer and warmer," she muttered as she wiped sweat off her brow with her forearm. She rearranged her bedding where her pillow rested against the new wall. She made her bed all the while scrutinizing her surroundings for something else to do. She unfolded another blanket and her mother's carrying pouch fell with a thump onto the made bed. She sighed as she unwrapped the most precious belonging, her father's bible. She searched for a special place to keep it and dragged an empty wood crate beside her mat, placed it upside down, and set one of her oil lamps on it. A place of honor as the first and last thoughts of her day. If the oil lasts, she could read it through the long, dark winter.

Readying herself for bed, she listened as the storm raged outside. She looked at the smoke hole, assured she had done the right thing. Despite the wind she had secured the flap with the pole and strapped the pole to the tipi. She had experienced storms many times and confidence in the experience assured her. One last thing before she slept, she would read her father's bible.

She couldn't remember where she and her mother had left off. It seemed months ago when the sickness had come to their village. Summer Sky unwrapped the waterproof leather her mother had kept it in and laid it beside the lamp on the crate.

She put a load of wood on the fire and crawled inside her warm sleeping furs.

"Lord, you are maker of heaven and earth. You sustain my every moment. And, if it is your will, my days are many and my life is long. I pray that I find my happiness with you alone. Even though I am still so lonely, you are with me. I could not do this without you, Lord."

Summer Sky picked up her father's bible and it fell open to Psalm Eight. She read, hoping it would ease her grief. She could hear her mother's voice in the words. Dispelling the sadness, she read aloud and made it personal.

"Lord, my God, the majesty and glory of your name fills all the earth and overflows the heavens. Through the praise of children and infants, you have established a stronghold against your enemies to silence the foe and the avenger. When I consider your heavens and see the work of your fingers, the moon, and the stars you have made, I cannot understand how you can bother with mere puny man or pay any attention to him.

"And yet you have made them a little lower than the angels and placed a crown of glory and honor upon his head. You have put them in charge of everything you have made, every living creature, every wild animal..." Summer Sky trailed off. "Lord, bless my traps, and I pray there is meat tomorrow."

Reading the bible aloud brought God closer as well as her mother. She closed the book, laid it aside on her makeshift nightstand, and turned down the wick on her oil lamp until it smoked and sputtered out. She slid deeper into her sleeping furs and stared at the flickering shadows the fire threw on the ceiling, contemplating the generosity of God.

CHAPTER SEVENTEEN

Something troubled Summer Sky. Everything seemed quiet and in order. Listening with intention while she stoked the fire, she added small twigs from her sorted pile. She blew on the embers, and they ignited with ease. As she added bigger sticks, she prepared her morning meal.

She poured warm water into her mug and drank, disappointed she'd run out of tea. She loved bee balm, but winter had killed it with the first frost. She'd settle for rosehips and the dried flower, bark, and leaves of the Ocean Spray bush, one of the few plants still accessible in winter. She looked forward to spring when strawberry and peppermint showed itself.

Summer Sky finished her breakfast and dressed. With her kettle in one hand, and her skillet in the other, she opened the flap of her tipi. Fresh snow and a cloud-spotted blue sky greeted her. When she stepped through the door, her heartbeat quickened. Wolf tracks, the size of her fist, circled her home in crisscross patterns. She looked across the white expanse searching for the wolf but saw nothing.

Summer Sky latched the door, and with knees rattling, she trekked toward the stream for more water and to clean her skillet. She followed the animal's tracks and scanned the woods for movement. Nothing. Instinct and the little hairs on the back of her neck told her it lurked somewhere close.

She couldn't hide in her tipi, crippled with fear of the beast in the woods. She must check her traps. Her survival depended on the meat. With determination, Summer Sky finished her task and tromped back. She put her pans away and grabbed the things she needed for a day outdoors, gathering what she could find for food.

With snowshoes, her bow, quiver, gathering bag, and her knife strapped on her belt, Summer Sky had prepared for anything. She crossed the frozen lake just below where the stream spilled into it and followed the animal trail created by the creatures seeking water throughout the dry seasons. It made for an easy snowshoe trek. At points though, the brush grew close along the stream, blocking her way around. It had made the perfect place for her traps.

At the first snare, she found nothing. She left it alone and moved on. Summer Sky reached a bench between two mountains where the woods opened into a small clearing. She stopped in mid stride as movement caught her eye. Her heart pounded. So strong, it gagged her. The wolf stood not but ten feet from her. In its mouth, the victim of her trap she had set the evening before. The stake and wire, still around its neck.

Anger and desperation welled up inside her. So angry and so hungry. That was her rabbit. Hers.

"Let it go. That's mine, you mangy thief. Get your own." Summer Sky screamed at the wolf. She screeched a war cry that grated on her throat as it escaped her lungs.

She pulled her bow off her shoulder and put an arrow onto the string in one swift movement. Sucking in a deep breath and letting it out, her untrained eye spied a spot on the wolf's chest just below the wilted rabbit dangling from its mouth.

The wolf just stood there, staring at her. It seemed unafraid of her. As she shouted at it, the wolf turned its head, first one way then the other as if it tried to understand her words. Summer Sky's thoughts about the creature tipped in her hasty labeling of it as an enemy. It too must survive the winter. But she narrowed in on the rabbit she so wanted in her stewpot. Her stomach growled, and so did she.

"Drop it." She commanded and tightened her pull on the bow string. She'd take its life for that rabbit. Before she could release the arrow, the wolf jumped with a midair turn and bounded into the forest, the rabbit flopping as it ran.

For some reason, Summer Sky no longer feared the wolf. If it planned on harming her, it would have done so already. She checked the rest of her snares and found only one other had tripped but remained empty. One set of tracks led away. Something had brushed against it, triggering it. She reset the wire, adjusting the position over the last tracks opening the mouth wider in hopes for meat tomorrow.

Summer Sky's failed attempt at trapping disappointed her but she refused to head back with nothing in her bag. Heading toward home, she gathered some pink leaves from a few huckleberry bushes, several handfuls of withered rosehips, and bunches of dried brown flowers along with bark and frost burned leaves of the ocean spray bush. No meat, though.

No meat and no Christmas celebration.

Sluffing off her belt, her bow and quiver, and her gathering bag just inside the door, Summer Sky's shoulders drooped as she settled in front of her fireless hearth. She went through the motions of building a fire without even a thought, the process so ingrained in her. Her mind focused on her empty stomach and the worry it caused her.

She searched for happy memories, replacing the despondent mood she found herself in. Her mind plagued by the wails of grief from the main lodge as people died and the gray face of her mother as she tied her into her grave clothes. By mid-afternoon, she pulled herself together and snagged her hatchet off the shelf by the door. Expending her frustrations, she hacked away at the other two logs outside her tipi.

As she chopped and split the wood then threw it by the door of her tipi, she wiped the cold tears that dripped off her nose and chin while she worked. A sob escaped, then another until she dropped into the snow.

"No, no, no, I can't do this. I want my mother back." She screamed into the evening sky. Her grip on the handle of the hatchet made her knuckles white. The blackness of her anger and fear contrasted with the beautiful pinks and violet of the setting sun. How could she go on like this? What should she do?

"Mama, why didn't you take me with you?" Summer Sky sobbed and rolled herself into a ball of grief on the snow. She pulled her knees up as she cried out her longing.

Just then a long, lonely howl came out of nowhere and everywhere. It reverberated against the rocky cliff and traveled along the snow until it reached Summer Sky. The sound mirrored her own grief. It brought on more sobs as she cried for the wolf as well. Perhaps the wolf grieved too?

Sniffling, Summer Sky realized how cold she had gotten lying in the snow outside her tipi. The sun had gone down, and the bitter night air seeped into her bones. She'd neglected the fire, and by now, it had gone out. Stiff, she stood, scooped up an armful of wood and headed inside.

She kept her parka on as she searched for a few coals. She gathered as many as she could find in a small pile, blowing on the glowing coals until they ignited the twigs, she had laid across them. The growl of her stomach washed another wave of grief over her as she prepared some oat cake batter, letting the salt of her sadness drop off her chin and into the bowl. Then, she buried a potato in the ashes under her fire. It'd take a few hours until the hot coals baked it. At least she had found the jar of rendered fat which would give her something of substance. But without meat her body couldn't withstand the cold, long, northwest winter.

While she waited for her potato, she nibbled on an oatcake. She had wasted an entire day dwelling on her despair. Her grief had wasted precious energy yet changed nothing.

As a sense of acceptance washed over her, she dug the potato out of the ashes and cut it open. She slathered fat onto it and watched it melt into a puddle on her plate. Summer Sky couldn't wait for the potato to cool and devoured it. She ignored the scalding of her tongue and licked the plate clean. Exhausted, she climbed into bed and gazed through the narrow opening of the smoke hole, watching the stars change.

"Mama, Papa, I love you," Summer Sky whispered.

CHAPTER EIGHTEEN

With rosehips and ocean-spray tea warming one hand, Summer Sky pushed open the door to watch the sunrise. There in front of her, lay a squirrel stretched out like a gift. A gift from a thieving wolf? The sorrowful howl she had heard the night before entered her mind. Had the wolf used a skinny squirrel as an offering, appeasing the screaming, crying human who had disrupted the quiet of his forest?

She looked closer and discerned the slight indentations in the packed snow of her trail. The wolf had come, dropped his gift, then left. Scanning the edge of the forest, she sensed it watching her. Strange, yet comforting.

"Thank you," Summer Sky whispered toward the forest.

"Thank you, Lord, for your provision. You work in strange and mysterious ways. I suppose this is not as strange as bread falling from the sky," She whispered and smiled.

She reached for the frozen carcass of the squirrel; it must have been laying there for some time. As she prepped, cleaned, and roasted the squirrel in the heat and smoke of her fire she contemplated the behavior of the wolf. The elders had never told a story of a wolf feeding a human that she could remember.

She took a bite of the wolf's gift and noticed the meat had a sweet and nutty flavor. Summer Sky pushed her manners aside as she picked every bit of the scant meat and sucked all the oils off each bone. It appeared she had just started eating her meal when it ended. Her hunger had only begun to ebb.

She wanted more. The small amount of sustenance won't hold off starvation. Not like a fat rabbit, had she reached her trap before that thief. Confusing emotions swirled around in her mind. Anger, frustration, fear, sadness, confusion, then acceptance for what she had no control over. The wolf had only done what wolves do. She must forgive him; but could they live together in the same territory? Summer Sky hoped for the best and prayed.

With her home completed, she focused on food. She pulled her skillet off the shelf and made oat cakes, mixing a bit of oats and a handful of wheat flour in the bowl along with a sparing, slight spoon of fat from the almost empty jar. Surveying the amount of flour, she had left, gauging she had enough for only a few more batches of oatcakes. She flattened out the sticky dough on her work bench and cut it into squares. Summer Sky dropped the delicate cakes into the hot pan on the coals of her fire. While she waited, she dressed to explore the cliff where she guessed her horses had found adequate shelter.

The oatcakes cooled as she wriggled into her mother's parka for the cold yet clear winter day. She took a moment to savor the scent and warmth of the fur surrounding the neck and hood. After Summer Sky secured the door flap, she stepped into her snowshoes and secured them onto her winter moccasin-clad feet. She slipped her food bag over her head and one arm, then did the same with the strap of her quiver of arrows making a crisscross across her chest. She fastened the belt which held the hatchet and a knife around the parka and prepared for whatever the day brought her.

As Summer Sky stepped away from her tipi, she scanned the surrounding area. She turned toward the frozen pond, then the hill below the cliff on the north and the stand of trees west of her. She studied each direction and listened; slight breeze moving through the treetops, the sound of crows cawing in the distance, a slight discernable trickle of water at the inlet of the lake. She stopped turning and held her breath, amplifying every sound. Tink, woosh, bubble, gurgle, the melody of nature's harmony whispered its presence. The morning had turned out beautiful, yet even the beavers had slept in, oblivious of the new day.

Just as she reached the water, she heard Wind approach with a whinny. He stood like a gentleman and allowed her and Sunshine a drink first. The horses wandered into the forest where they could find more accessible grass under the trees. She let them go and headed toward the cliff following the trail the horses had made.

They had traveled for water many times which marked the way up the side of the cliff. She would have had difficulty finding it otherwise. It amazed her that the horses seemed comfortable on such a narrow route.

The path made a slight corner where the cliff curved inward. Summer Sky couldn't see ahead of her. It looked like a dead end. Around the corner it widened, there she found it in a cleft of the rock, the mouth of a cave as tall as a horse and twice as wide. No wonder she couldn't see it from her camp. It angled toward the west.

She turned, scanned the horizon, and gasped at the view. The beauty spread out for miles with layers of snow-crusted, tree-covered mountains. The distant layer, a little bit smaller than the one in front. The mountains seemed endless, but somewhere below her, the river cut through the layers of mountains. She stood admiring the vista in front of her, until her curiosity got the better of her.

Summer Sky stepped toward the opening of the cave and noticed hoof prints in the dry clay floor. Entering, she dragged her hand across the jagged rock which copied the outer surface of the cliff. The light of the morning sun had not reached the gap of the cave opening. She noticed faded markings, left there by her mother's people, on smooth sections before her. It comforted her that generations of the People had existed in this region for centuries. Despite the great sickness, the People would live, find new loved ones, and make new families. Life would go on.

But not for a native daughter with blue eyes. With sadness and longing flowing through her constricted breath, Summer Sky stretched out her bare hand and touched an ancient drawing on the cave wall. She traced the bold brush strokes across the cold, solid surface of the rock and wondered about the artist. Dwelling on the past people who had used this cave brought her own past and even her uncertain future into focus. She sighed and turned back toward the cave opening.

She traveled the path she had seen heading up the cliff. The horse's tracks went in that direction as well, so she followed them. The cliff-edged trail took her up a wider, less steep slope which helped Summer Sky relax. She preferred the enclosing branches of a tree lined path surrounding her in their security over the exposure of the open cliff trail. Exposed and cold on that rock, she stepped up her pace, getting off the ledge as soon as possible.

By the time she reached the top, Summer Sky had warmed from the exertion. She had entered a meadow. She could tell the horses had grazed there by the patches of grass uncovered and pulled up by the roots.

Then, she saw the paw prints of the wolf and feared for her horses when they came for food. Could they end up food themselves by grazing with their heads down and not paying attention? Scanning the area for any danger, Summer Sky walked in circles reading the prints in the snow. Every trail led toward the edge of the cliff overlooking her camp. So, the critter had been watching her every move.

When she turned, she noticed the pawprint of the wolf covering a print of a different animal. Summer Sky bent over and examined it closer. The ridges between the wolf's four toes crumbled when she touched them. It could still be in the area. The owner of the other much bigger print under it, she gauged as older. It could be hours or even days older. She studied the larger and wider footprint closer. She couldn't see nails. It had four toes like the wolf, but the wolf pawprint would show its nails.

Recognition dawned as she straightened. Mountain Lion. The mountain lion's claws retracted until they attacked. In one motion she had her bow in her left hand and an arrow ready. A mountain lion, especially in winter when the deer and elk migrated below the frost line, would attack a horse. She worried about her horses and headed toward the path back down.

I know those tracks are older than the wolf's but how much older. A week, a few days, this morning? The hair on the back of her neck stood, tickling her skin. She stopped, on high alert.

"Lord, I pray the tracks are days or weeks old. Please...." Her prayer dropped off with an intake of breath.

Then, she saw it. It stood between her and her escape. Her eyes darted in every direction, searching for a different route. Her heart skipped a beat as she held her breath then it sped up. She adjusted her stance with her left foot forward. A trickle of sweat slid down the side of her face.

She pulled her bow tight. She couldn't falter and would not contemplate her lack of skill with the bow at this time. The cat lowered its head and stared at her. She quelled her panic and hoped the breeze might rush the smell of her fear away from the lion. It stood at a distance, far enough away. She would have plenty of warning if it should charge.

Summer Sky stood her ground. "Please, go away," she whispered as she dropped her left hand off her bow and pulled her knife from its sheath at her belt. Bringing it up with her bow, she held both at the same time. If she missed with the arrow, she could use her knife. She may survive if her knife landed a killing blow.

A husky growl came from the cat's wide-open mouth. Summer Sky's knees shook. The wild animal paced across the snowshoe tracks she had made earlier as if claiming territory. It didn't look away once. A bad sign. The arrow clattered against the bow as Summer Sky trembled from the exertion of holding it taut. She searched in vain for an open target on the animal, but it kept pacing. She dreaded the moment it would charge.

She stepped back, maybe she could find another way down off the cliff. Maybe the mountain lion would consider her less of a threat if she moved away. She tangled her snowshoes and lost her balance, falling onto her right hip. She still had a hold of her bow and knife, but the arrow disappeared into the snow.

She heard her pounding heartbeat throbbing in her ears as she watched the beast moving closer. Her right hand reached for another arrow. Out of the edge of her vision she saw a grey streak bounding toward her. It scattered powdered ice crystals into the air with each powerful stride. She couldn't fight off both predators. Her fate sealed.

"Mama, I'll see you soon." Summer Sky braced for the impact from her right, but it didn't come.

She opened her eyes at a growl in front of her. The wolf stood between her and the menacing cat. The mountain lion roared. It echoed through the meadow as it charged. The wolf met its opponent in mid-stride. The screams and snarls filled the small meadow. Summer Sky's head spun in confusion and disbelief. Her heart hammered so fast in her chest. Her lungs couldn't keep up. She scrambled onto her feet and secured another arrow.

Blood speckled the white meadow as the two fought. Summer Sky inched toward the side of the scene and hoped she'd get down the path before the battle ended. Too late, the wolf dropped, and the mountain lion stood over it. No, the wolf had it by the neck and wouldn't let go. Summer Sky took the chance, she pulled on her bowstring, narrowed her gaze onto a small place just behind the front leg. The perfect angle. She stretched the arrow string toward her chin, exhaled, and let the arrow fly.

The arrowhead sunk into the fur at the place where she had aimed, the cat faltered, then dropped. Summer Sky stood in shock with another arrow hanging from her limp right arm. Just then the whinny of horses came from below. The two popped out at the top of the trail and came running, snorting from the frantic climb up the narrow path.

Her knees collapsed, and she toppled over.

"Lord God in Heaven, thank you for my life. And thank you for the life of that wolf. Why did he do that?"

As the survival instinct drained from her, she struggled onto her feet. Sticky with sweat.

"Don't fall apart now." Summer Sky clung onto Wind's neck and took deep breaths. She had won. The wolf saved her life. What a wonder. Gratitude came out in a cry of thanks and sadness. It had given its life for her. Her cry turned into keening from so much loss. In the wilderness she had nothing holding her back. She let it out into the sky, the trees, and her beloved horses who stood above her in their ever-patient way.

Gaining her composure with several deeper breaths, her attention on the pile of fur-covered lives spilled out onto the frigid mountain meadow. She must see her champion. Gaining her feet, she scuffled through the bloodied field and shoved the dead mountain lion off the wolf. He had let go of the cat's neck, her hope that he survived dashed. He would only let go in death. But then he took a breath.

Gratitude burst through the aftermath of the adrenalin coursing through her body. Gratitude toward this crazy animal that protected her for no apparent reason. Kneeling at the side of the wolf, she wiped tears from her eyes as she examined her wounded hero.

The wolf lived but needed attention. Her trained eye followed the long gash on its side.

"Wind, here boy." Summer Sky called her horse, as she reached into her food pouch for a scoop of crumbled oatcakes. She must have smashed them when she fell. Wind pawed at the snow with his head down. She clicked her tongue in a way that calmed him, and he stepped closer. She held out her hand and showed him what she had. He came, laid his warm muzzle into her palm, and licked up the crumbs.

"I need you and Sunshine." He snorted as if in disbelief at what she asked of him, and she smiled.

"That's a good boy. You will help me carry the wolf back so I can fix him up. Sunshine will carry the mountain lion. Or would you prefer the big cat?" Wind looked at Sunshine as if they argued in the silent language of horses.

Summer Sky stepped toward the wolf as if Wind would follow but instead, he stepped in front of her and shoved her back with his big head. She gained her balance by bracing herself against his shoulder and shoved back.

"You will do this. I need you to do this." Summer Sky wrapped her arms around Wind's neck and leaned into him until he stepped back. Her mother had taught her this trick of gaining control, but in a loving way. She led him toward the side of the panting and bleeding wolf. She heaved with all the strength she had. Her muscles shaking to the point of collapse as she draped the nearly unconscious beast across Wind's back. She couldn't leave Wind alone with it while she loaded up the mountain lion, so she tied a rawhide strap around the cat's front legs and had Sunshine drag it down the cliff trail behind her.

With a hand shielding her eyes, she looked at the sky. "It's only mid-morning," she told Wind. She still had several hours of daylight, which gave her plenty of time to process her first kill as well as take care of the wolf's injuries. The death lock the wolf had had on the lion's neck still astonished her. Regardless, she had meat. Summer Sky smiled as she imagined herself coaxing the wolf with an oatcake the way she had done with the horses.

CHAPTER NINETEEN

Summer Sky's strange clan arrived at her camp with the unconscious wolf draped over an unhappy horse. Sunshine had dragged the dead mountain lion through the knee-deep snow by its front legs. With the exertion and fright from the event in the meadow, her hunger swelled for more than a crumbled oatcake. She longed for a sizable chunk of the mountain lion roasting in her oven and her mouth watered at the thought. Even though she preferred elk or deer, her worries of starvation had subsided.

Torn between caring for the wolf's injuries or getting meat roasting, she hesitated. She doubted he would manage more than broth for a while. Organ meat had nutrients which would help in healing. Before she did anything else, Summer Sky took her pot from the firepit and emptied her water bag into it, then set it in the coals.

She grabbed her butcher knife; she would gather the heart and liver from the mountain lion. Without squirming, she sawed into the frozen hide of its belly, avoiding the intestines and placed the organs in the snow. She hesitated for a slight moment staring into the opened corpse, she couldn't resist taking a section of the shoulder and getting it roasting while she stitched up the wolf's side.

Anxious for her patient, breathing sporadic near the door of her tent, she wiped her hands in the snow, cleaning off as much of the mountain lion blood as she could. The light outside would work best. She wished she'd had her outdoor firepit built, but she would make do.

Carrying the meat inside she placed the roast in her oven and buried it in the coals alongside the steaming pot of organ meat and its broth. Another delay, she needed the fire built up so the roast would cook for a long time. When she finished the surgery, she would eat.

She heaped wood between the two pots and laid a bed for the wolf near her work bench. Hurrying, she gathered her tools and the fur sled so she could easily move him without hurting him further. She also grabbed a cup of the steaming broth, added powdered yarrow root and a good portion of chamomile leaves, then headed for her patient.

Acid bubbled up from her stomach, burning her throat as she stepped outside. So much could go wrong, and she had never sutured anyone before, only watched. Would it be like sewing a hide together making clothing or repairing her tipi? She would soon find out.

Summer Sky knelt beside the panting wolf and examined his side. The jagged gash punctured the skin just below the bottom rib and scraped across each one, exposing three ribs, before grazing the shoulder. She reached for his hind leg checking for more wounds, but he yelped and pulled away. She must calm him. Frightened, she moved toward his head humming a quiet tune hoping it would soothe him.

"I will help you, my friend. As you helped me. Please, let me help you." Summer Sky reached her hand toward his head so he could sniff her.

"You're all right. This will hurt, but if I don't do it you will die. Please don't die." She set the chamomile thickened organ meat broth in front of him. He opened an eye and stared at her. Summer Sky sensed he measured her with that one look.

"You can trust me." Summer Sky whispered while she dipped her finger into the broth and dribbled it onto his snout. His tongue slipped from his mouth and cleaned up the mess.

"Good boy." Summer Sky smiled and dipped and dribbled several times before the wolf must have decided to end this boring game. He stuck his face into the bowl and finished the broth. With a sigh, the wounded animal fell back on his side and rested easier.

Summer Sky moved beside the wolf and continued the examination discovering the animal, in fact, was female and not male. And concern filled her further as she noticed the wolf's bottom two teats had milk in them. She had pups.

She must move fast. Summer Sky would save this wolf for more reasons than that it had protected her. She must save the pups in return for the wolf's sacrifice. Summer Sky checked the wolf for any signs of resistance, but the chamomile had worked. She stepped inside for garlic water, warm water from her kettle, and a soft flannel rag for cleaning the wound. Then, she laid out her supplies near the wolf in order of importance. Wetting the rag with warm water she wiped away the drying blood from the gaping wound. Then she used the entire quart jar of garlic water and washed away loose hair and shredded skin. The lucky she-wolf's battle with the mountain lion hadn't damaged anything more than skin. Despite being deep, a simple box stitch would suffice.

With shaking hands Summer Sky threaded her mother's special curved needle. She pinched the two sides of the gash together with her cold left hand and laid her first stitch, tying it in a double box knot the way her mother had taught her and snipped the ends. She repeated the stitch until she finished at the wolf's shoulder, her fingers white with cold. She would have failed if the wolf hadn't kept them from freezing.

Next, Summer Sky went back inside and prepared a poultice. She reached for the dried pitch of the western hemlock tree her mother had ground into a fine powder.

Sprinkling a good portion of the jar into a stone bowl, she added usnea and yarrow, grounding them together with a pestle. Then she made a paste, mixing the last bit of garlic water into the Medicinals until it had the consistency of pottery clay. She took the bowl outside, grabbing a roll of flannel off the storage shelf just inside the door.

"How are you feeling my friend?" Checking for a reaction, she called out in a soft, sing song voice. She lowered herself in one slow, gentle motion. The wolf hadn't flinched and remained under the effects of the chamomile and loss of blood.

Summer Sky worked fast so she could get the wolf moved in before she woke up. She scooped a portion of poultice paste with her fingers, spread it across the entire wound, and wrapped cotton flannel material around the ribs and shoulder, tying it behind her neck so she couldn't reach the knot. She would keep a close watch on her patient while the wound healed.

Summer Sky moved the pitiful thing onto the sled and stopped at the door of the warm tipi. She worried about jostling her patient over the raised threshold. With a deep breath, she hefted the wolf with both arms under the fur so she wouldn't disturb the stitches, and the wolf stayed asleep. She dragged her patient near the wall behind her workbench.

She gathered a blanket off her bed and laid it over the wolf, leaving her patient on the fur sled for now. Summer Sky watched the wolf breathe in and out. She stood there wondering how long the chamomile would keep the animal asleep, then she smelled the roast and her stomach growled.

She finished preparing it with a valuable dried carrot and a chopped-up potato. She ate, her hunger took precedence as she bit into the crunchy potato chunks and chewed a tough slice of mountain lion. Still, not her favorite meat.

With her belly full, she must do something with the carcass of the mountain lion outside, before it attracts more predators. She grabbed her butcher knife and saw, then headed out the door with her snowshoes. She had kept the rope tied around the legs and roped it around her shoulder and middle. She dragged the body toward the woods nearby, then climbed a sturdy tree with the free end of the rope. Pulling the huge cat into the air, it made the harvest of the meat and hide easier.

The way of her mother's people, using everything, honored her mother and the mountain lion's life. The fur would keep her warm, especially fortunate taking it down in winter. The bones for tools or fuel since it burned hot and slow. Summer Sky used the intestines for sewing and suturing, the stomach for storing food and water. The organ meat broth would help in the recovery of the wolf and the meat would keep them fed, along with the marrow and bones for broth.

The rest would feed the hungry critters like racoons and skunks and porcupines in the area. She left it hanging in the tree to freeze and would come back for the rest later. She dropped the meat and marrow bones onto the mountain lion hide and dragged the bundle back toward her tipi for prepping and drying over the smoky fire in the rafters of her home.

She cleaned up the mess near the front of her tipi with her father's shovel. With her hands grasping the tool her vision blurred, and her heart ached. The motion transported her back into the hole she had dug for her mother's grave. With her sore, tired heart she scooped the bloody snow into a bucket and dumped it in the woods away from her doorway.

Passing her home with the shovel and empty bucket she went to the stream, rinsed them, then got fresh water for bathing herself after the bloody day. Summer Sky squatted and reached the trickle from the spring. She noticed the dried blood under her fingernails and the stains down the front of her coat. She scrunched her nose in regret at what she had worn. She hoped her mother's parka would come clean.

CHAPTER TWENTY

Throughout the night, Summer Sky mixed chamomile, dried yarrow root, willow bark, and arnica into her mortar. She crushed the ingredients for pain relief together with some organ broth. At intervals, the wolf whimpered, the pain evident in her cry. She dribbled broth medicine onto the wolf's snout enticing her awake long enough to finish the bowl and settle into a more restful sleep.

Summer Sky lay in her bed watching the smoke from her fire weave its way through the rack of mountain lion meat, cut into strips and hung over the fire. Smoke cured the meat, drying it for the weeks and months ahead. But would the meat last? And how long would she have this strange house guest? She had trouble trusting the wild animal and must find a better place for her in the morning, but for now keeping her sleepy with medicinal herbs helped Summer Sky relax some.

Animals, including wolves, had an instinct about the healing properties of plants. When they fell ill, they searched specific plants out and ate them, or rolled around in them. But Summer Sky understood, by the deepness of the wound, the wolf wouldn't have survived without her care. But in her home? Reluctant, she took her eyes off the animal and imagined all the things that could go wrong, including waking with the beast's fangs digging into her throat.

Her eyes drooped, then flew open, searching for protection. She gathered her bow, quiver, and knife, then brought them near her sleeping platform. She placed the knife on the stand beside her bed. The bow and quiver she hung on the half wall at the head of her sleeping pallet.

Still fidgeting, Summer Sky stoked the fire and added wood, then set her kettle in the coals. Yes, a wolf in her tipi seemed like a poor plan. She made herself some calming lavender tea and sipped. Just as sleep carried her into dreams, a noise crept in, and she sat up grabbing her knife. Something had scraped against the door and snorted. Concerned, she clambered out of her sleeping furs and went toward the door. Wind had shown up for some reason.

Summer Sky, with her heart hammering against her ribs, stood at the door. She opened the flap. The horse pushed her out of the way and came into her home. He searched around until he found the wolf asleep, then let out a huff.

Confusion wrapped her mind, until Wind moved near and pulled her in with his big head. Wind must share her worries about the wolf. This touched Summer Sky and a misty-eyed sniffle escaped as she wrapped her arms around her dearest friend and sighed.

"You want to stay in here and protect me, huh my big friend?" She scratched Wind between the ears then laid her forehead against his.

Turning, she leaned her back against his shoulder. Summer Sky searched for a place for her big, jealous horse. She could almost laugh except she realized his protective jealousy had come from the bond the two had formed out of pain and grief. He had witnessed every painful event of her young life. Yes, of course she would let him stay inside with her.

She chose a place as far away from the wolf as possible in the small, confined space of her home. She pushed aside her storage baskets and made a partial barrier between her sleeping pallet and the wolf, then made a space for him near her bed. Wind moved through the interior avoiding the obstacles of the fire pit and dangling meat. With a grunt, he settled on the floormat Summer Sky had rolled out for him. He turned toward her and gave her a long look then studied the wolf. Wind stayed alert as she checked on the patient.

Her horse's presence comforted her. She crawled back into

bed, yawned, and snuggled down in her still warm covers. Sleep would give her a reprieve from the tension and stress of the day, at least until the next whimper alerted her that her patient needed more pain medicine.

*   *   *

The night dragged on. With every movement she made, she heard Wind shift on the dry grass mat. Her ever-vigilant guard. The wolf, oblivious of her surroundings, traveled her healing journey through a deep sleep.

Summer Sky shot out of bed in the early morning light when she heard a low growl and hoof stomping. She had her bow armed with an arrow, ready for battle. She must win this battle. She set her weapons down and moved between the combatants with her hands open.

"Shush you two, we are all friends here." Summer Sky said in a low tone hoping it would calm the strained nerves of her house guests.

The wolf rose from her mat. Summer Sky guessed she felt vulnerable. Wind stepped between her and the wolf, but the crowded space limited his movement and he backed into the baskets, toppling them over. The contents spilled out toward the fire. Summer Sky dove for the items. The wolf yelped standing on wabbling legs and growled at them both.

Wind pounded his feet in warning and lunged at the wolf, shoving Summer Sky, and rushing past her. She stumbled and fell hard on the edge of her firepit wall. Pain shot through her hip as she stood. Summer Sky must rescue herself this time or Wind would trample her. What could she do? She watched the wolf hold her stance. Her entire body shook with effort. The wolf's head swiveled as if she couldn't decide which of them posed the greater threat.

Wind acted as if he would kill the wolf, he had a crazy look in his eyes. Summer Sky must gain control before they destroyed her home, but how?

Years ago, Summer Sky had watched her uncle train Wind with a firm and low tone of voice. She communicated with her soft voice most of the time, but this called for dominance, or her world may change again, for the worse.

"Wind, no." Summer Sky scolded and pushed herself between them again. She grabbed a rope that hung on the corner of the workbench and slung it over her horses back, snagging the end as it swung under Wind's neck.

"Settle," she said as she pulled down on the rope, repeating the action until she had backed Wind toward the door. She looked over her shoulder at the wolf still standing on unstable legs with her head drooping. The wolf locked her eyes on the two of them standing at the door.

"Now look you two, we must find some common ground here, mortal enemies or not. Both of you settle down." She backed away from Wind and opened the door. Morning rays of sunshine slanted through her door. She pointed at the opening and watched as Wind lowered his head and left.

"You, lie down right now before you break open your stitches." Summer Sky made a sign pushing her palm down toward the floor. She hoped the wolf would understand her stern voice and the hand sign. The wolf seemed unsure for a moment.

"Lie down, please." She said with a quieter voice but still standing firm using the hand signal again. The wolf panted and shook before her legs gave out with a huff and laid back down but kept a keen watch on the door.

Summer Sky followed Wind and put her arms around his neck, she understood his mood.

"Now you go get your breakfast. I will take care of our guest. This is important. That wolf saved my life, and I will save hers. Go on, now." Summer Sky shooed Wind away. She grabbed her kettle and headed toward the spring for fresh water, giving the wolf some space.

When she entered the tipi, Summer Sky noticed the wolf had moved off the fur sled. She placed the kettle on the firepit wall and built a fire. She ignored the wolf as she prepared broth for her new friend.

The wolf had barricaded itself under the workbench and with frantic eyes watched Summer Sky while it licked the flannel bandage. The pitiful thing must be in pain. As she kept an eye on the wolf, she searched her mind for the healing herbs that might soothe her patient's fears.

As the tea kettle steamed, she closed her eyes and recalled a long past memory of her mother at the workbench. Taking deep breaths combatting the ache in her chest, she focused on what her mother had used on a woman who'd spilled boiling soup on her lap, scalding her thigh.

Her mother had used the usual things; garlic water, arnica, aloe vera for soothing the burn, but what had she used for pain and calmness? Summer Sky searched the shelves. All the jars had labels but had she and her mother thought of writing the remedies on the jars, she could locate them much easier. Right now, she must find... she spotted a jar with seeds in it labeled cow parsnip. She found the ingredients she needed for a fresh poultice. The seeds of the flower, when crushed, calmed the damaged nerves. But what could she use to calm the wolf's fears and help it sleep?

She set the seeds on the work bench and kept searching. Transported into the past, another memory surfaced.

"But mama, why do they hate me?" Summer Sky recalled the tearful conversation with her mother.

"They only know what they know, honey. They know brown eyes. Your blue eyes worry them and make them uncomfortable, so they lash out. It's not you they fear, you're a little girl. They'll come around," Water Lily said as she wiped her little girl's face with a washcloth dipped in warm water. The children hurt her feelings more than they hurt her physically, but still her emotional scars ran deep.

Her mother had made her a tea of purple flowers and leaves, she recalled the dried flowers floating and how it made her heart soften so that she could sleep and forget the painful taunting.

She searched for the jar of dried purple flowers and in the back, she found it. On the label she read Blue Vervain. She counted a few in the jar. She wondered if her mother had soothed grief during the terrible sickness. Now, Summer Sky would calm a terrified wolf and get the wild beast comfortable staying in a tipi with a human. Hopefully, the remedy would calm her enough, keeping her from tearing at the bandages, then the stitches.

Finishing the grinding of the cow parsnip seeds along with yarrow, usnea, arrow leaf balsam leaves and some yarrow root for the poultice, she started on the broth. She pounded pieces of meat into a paste, then stirred it in, making it easier for her patient's stomach.

The wolf's body must focus on healing instead of digesting. Summer Sky arranged the items to replace the wolf's dressing, but first the broth. She took the bowl with the purple flowers of the blue vervain crushed in along with arnica, chamomile, and yarrow root toward the wolf. She hoped the added meat would hide the bitter taste of the yarrow root now that the wolf seemed more alert.

"Are you ready for some food? Here you go." Summer Sky set the bowl down beside the wolf, stepped back and sat cross legged a couple of feet away. If the wolf became accustomed to her scent, her nearness wouldn't trouble her while she changed the bandages.

The wolf acted as if she would push herself further under the workbench, but the meat scent wafted into the air, and she caught sight of the bowl. She looked at Summer Sky then back at the bowl.

"Good girl, eat your breakfast." Summer Sky reached in slow motion and slid the bowl closer so that the wolf could remain in her hiding place. But the animal did scoot out a bit. Summer Sky matched each movement keeping the same distance between them as the wolf came forward until she had gained her feet.

The wolf lapped up the meal and licked the bowl then

looked at Summer Sky as if thanking her. Summer Sky moved, feigning getting up, but the wolf bent her legs, ready for an attack or bolt for the door. She stopped and stared the wolf down. With slow movements she stretched out her hand palm down so the wolf could sniff her. She just stared back with her head cocked as if confused by Summer Sky's actions.

Summer Sky studied the animal's golden eyes and cocked her head, mimicking the wolf. It turned her head the other way. The girl and the wolf played this game until the girl broke out in a joy filled laugh.

"You are a funny thing, little sister." Summer Sky reached again. The wolf's tongue fell out of her mouth, and she panted. She imagined the wolf had laughed too. Then, she stopped panting and stepped toward Summer Sky with her head down. Could it mean the wolf had submitted? She froze but smiled and cooed at the wolf, encouraging her.

The wolf's legs trembled after three steps, and she dropped with a whimper so heartbreaking.

"Poor baby, such a good girl. You're all right. I will help you." Summer Sky soothed with her soft voice as she inched closer until she sat beside her panting patient. She put her hand near the wolf's nose, then with the other hand she petted the side of her snout and gave her ear a scratch. She had lived around enough dogs and had learned they liked their ears scratched. Wolves and dogs were relatives. The wolf's condition had kept the animal from objecting as the effects of the potent medicine calmed the anxiety and took the pain away.

She kept petting until the wolf had fallen into a deep sleep, then with scissors, she snipped the old bandage off and examined the wound for signs of infection like swelling and discoloration. She brought her oil lamp over for better light.

Summer Sky noticed slight swelling between the stitches, which seemed normal after one day. Pink in color and not too red. When she pushed the stitches, they held with no seepage, this pleased her. The wolf healed fast. How long could she keep the wolf sedated so she wouldn't run away? How long must the stitches stay in? Better the stitches stay in for at least seven days. Could she keep the wolf happy that long?

Summer Sky spread the poultice paste across the stitches and rewrapped the wound with a new bandage. She sat with the wolf and continued petting her head and the side of her neck. She gauged the ruckus, the preparing of the medicine and the actual changing of the dressing took until mid-morning. She couldn't tell through the smoke hole with the meat dangling there. The short winter day had turned sunless and cold.

As Summer Sky watched the sleeping wolf, the lack of sleep hit her. Her body became weighted as if filled with sand. The night before had caught up with her. Scooting over near the fire, she stoked it and added more wood. Surprised when the flames flared, she got goosebumps along her arms. She had intervened in the argument, calmed everyone down, and doctored the poor beast all while in her night dress. Cold had long ago seeped into her bones, but because she had other priorities, she hadn't noticed.

She added more wood, building the flames higher in hopes it would warm her faster. She pulled her sleeping furs off her bed and around her shoulders, then sat in front of her firepit. Not enough. The fire couldn't warm her fast enough.

She pulled her sleeping mat over and curled up on it, shivering. Reaching her hand out of her fur she brought the warm kettle against her body under the fur. This helped. As the shivering stopped, she thought about breakfast for herself. But first she would dress in her warmest inside clothing.

She made and ate breakfast in slow motion. She drank her tea, still snuggled up on her sleeping mat then watched the wolf for any signs she would wake soon. The wolf breathed deep and rhythmic. That type of sleep would last awhile. She imagined the morning took a toll on her patient. She should take a nap herself. She stoked the fire, adding more wood and laid down facing the wolf, if the animal stirred, she would awaken.

CHAPTER TWENTY-ONE

Summer Sky leaned against the most recent improvement. While her patient had slept at intervals during her healing process, Summer Sky and the horses had moved enough rock from the cliff for an outdoor firepit. The building project had slowed between nursing her patient and taking care of herself. As the warmth of the rocks penetrated her winter layers, she watched the beavers scurry around their home. She sipped her morning tea of rosehips and huckleberry leaves while winter sunshine, defying the cold, warmed her face.

"Thank you, Lord, for your provision. Thank you for my health and courage for tackling the hard things that frighten me." Summer Sky breathed in the crisp air and let it out on a long exhale. She had struggled with forming a routine without the constant threat of emergencies. The frantic burden of not knowing what would happen next exhausted her. She appreciated the quiet morning where she could relax and enjoy her tea.

While the wolf slept with the door of the tipi open in case her recovering patient joined the day outside, Summer Sky watched the white cotton clouds move, unhurried, across the blue expanse above. She wished she could emulate the clouds. She hung her kettle of water on an iron arm over the new firepit and planned a bath on a much-needed rest day.

Summer Sky had also neglected the counting stick. While she waited for the bath water, she picked it up and counted the last day she had marked.

"The day of the mountain lion," she mused.

"Five days. No, six. I missed Christmas."

No matter how late, she would celebrate anyway. Renewed plans washed a flood of excited energy over her.

"So much for a restful day." She laughed, pushed herself away from the warm firepit wall and stood. Summer Sky entered the tipi and checked on the wolf.

The animal slept, peacefully in the corner between the worktable and the wall. She grabbed the saw and gathering pouch along with her digging tools. With the hide sled draped over her shoulder, she set out on her snowshoes toward the forest. The frozen mountain lion carcass hanging in the tree, her first stop. The mountain lion's death had meaning, it had brought food and healing.

When she reached the tree where the mountain lion carcass hung, she stood, staring, confused. What had happened? The rope hung in the tree limp, swaying in the breeze with no animal attached. Something had gnawed through the rope and dragged the thing away. She had lost so much meat. She had taken only the thicker and fattier portions. She had hoped that once the wolf had healed enough, she would harvest the rest of the mountain lion meat.

Overwhelming despair brought panic bubbling up her throat, closing it off from air. They wouldn't survive the winter. The realization slammed against her like a physical force, and her knees buckled. For Christmas she would have given her new friend something special. A bag of rib bones with some meat still on them for starters.

"Lord, you supply my every need. I trust in you." The pressure in her lungs and her throat eased. She wrapped what remained of the rope around her arm.

She searched the area for signs of what had taken the carcass. Over the snow and her previous snowshoe tracks, laid out a crisscross pattern of large wolf prints. Another wolf in their midst? What could this mean for their safety? And her patient, could she be in danger once she hunted again? Would another of her kind accept her or harm her since she had the smell of a human on her? The pounding of her heart signaled her fear, and she scanned the trees, assuring her safety. She turned toward camp empty-handed and filled with worry.

* * *

What would she do? For days the question dogged her as she went about her chores. She must increase her efforts with the traps she set every evening and checked every morning. Why she rarely caught anything confused her. If she had been a boy, the elders would have taken turns training the fatherless child as a hunter.

When she returned, she found the wolf lying beside the outside firepit with her head on her paws, as if waiting for her. Her head popped up and she wagged her tail when Summer Sky broke out of the trees. The site lightened her spirits for a moment. She would not rest easy unless they found food.

"Are you feeling better, little sister?" The animal wagged her tail without whimpering.   Smiling, Summer Sky thought about giving the wolf a name for Christmas. It seemed the only gift she had to give. She had gotten in the habit of calling her "little sister" in her mind.

"Little Sister? Is that a good name for you?" Summer Sky called out in greeting. The wolf's mouth dropped open, and her tongue flopped out in what looked like a grin.

The day before, Summer Sky had noticed Little Sister had bounded toward her when she entered camp. She noted the submission and regarded it as a God-sent present for herself, but she wouldn't take it for granted. Yes, the animal saved her life and in return Summer Sky had saved the wolf, but had she trained the wildness out of Little Sister? Like taming the horses? Once she freed the wolf of the stitches, it could go.

Since the wound had healed enough, the time had come. Little Sister may leave soon after. Summer Sky would miss her company, but she'd rejoice the wolf still lived.

"Hey, hey, Little Sister." Summer Sky left the empty sled at the tipi and with sadness she put her tools away and hung her empty foraging bag on the peg by the door. Leaving the tipi, she sat by the firepit and stoked the flames, pushing the unburnt ends inward with a skill borne from years of experience. The wolf watched her with her head tilted as if she read Summer Sky's sadness.

"Lay down, my friend." She encouraged with a hand signal, and the wolf settled down beside her for an ear scratching.

"Good girl, now let me see those stitches. I bet they itch something terrible." Summer Sky imagined cutting the sutures free while the wolf scratched, bit, and pushed her away. She must sedate her again; she hoped for the last time.

She whistled for the horses and waited with Little Sister. She placed wood in the firepit and blew on the coals. The uncertainties within herself swam around in her head until she could take no more. She must find food, but for now she needed a break from her needs. For the time being, Summer Sky would enjoy the beautiful winter day with her friends, without worrying about anything.

The horses came down from the cliff. When they saw the wolf with her, they kept their distance, still distrustful around Little Sister. She must join them if she wanted to share in the giving of the blessing of Christ's birth. Reaching inside the door she grabbed the curry brush off the shelf, a bag of special items she had saved for the occasion, and a comb. She fastened the door behind her. The wolf could spend the day outdoors or join them in the meadow above.

The sun had melted the top layer of snow, compacting it on the trail leading to the cliff, making the trek easy and fast. Summer Sky met the horses at the bottom and glanced back at camp. The wolf had followed. Summer Sky noted the stitches had healed well, recalling her first-hand knowledge of stitch healing. They would come out today, but first for some fun.

With a smile and a whistle, Summer Sky motioned for the wolf to join them in the meadow. She petted Sunshine and Wind while she waited for the wolf, encouraging the horses to accept this one predator.

"Little Sister is part of our odd pack now, so be kind." She hoped the mortal enemies might find common ground and live together in peace, at least for the time being. The wolf slunk up beside Summer Sky, acting shy of the horses.

Unlacing her snowshoes, she tied them on her bag and slung them onto Wind's back, then she grabbed a handful of his mane, and swung herself up. Riding might be easier if she kept her eyes closed on the narrow part of the cliffside trail.

CHAPTER TWENTY-TWO

Their party of four had reached the meadow above the camp. The sobering view of the tracks and blood from the battle with the mountain lion retold the story across the snow-covered field. New snow hadn't yet erased the evidence. The skin on Wind's shoulder rippled when she laid a soft hand on him in comfort. Summer Sky studied the other two animals. Sunshine stomped, and Little Sister whined.

But Little Sister seemed the most agitated. She whimpered and paced.

"What's wrong, girl?" Summer Sky slid off Wind's back and put her snowshoes on. Could the wolf's movements on the first long trip out cause her to pull on her stitches? Reaching for the distressed animal, Little Sister placed her snout in the girl's open hand. The wolf whined again and paced, then ran in the same direction she had on the day she saved Summer Sky's life.

"Wait," She called, and the wolf stopped, gave her a long look as if communicating something important, then trotted back. Little Sister yipped, grabbed the hem of Summer Sky's parka with her teeth, and pulled with a gentle tug.

"You want me to come with you?" The wolf turned and walked in front of Summer Sky, looking back at regular intervals. The horses trailed behind them at a slower pace as they dug in the sun-softened snow for their breakfast.

Little Sister led her toward the edge of the open space and into the trees. Tufts of tall grass poked through the snow. Between the sparce brush and stunted trees lay rocky outcrops at the foot of a shale covered hillside. A concealed den, noticeable from the perfect angle, lay hidden at the side of a hill. Little Sister's home had natural camouflage with rocks and bushes. Summer Sky would have missed it had she not had the wolf as a guide.

"Clever mama."

Around the hole in the piled rocks, she read a struggle in the snow. The wolf paced and whined. Summer Sky knelt and put her arms around the wolf's neck. They cried together. The mountain lion tracks concentrated at the mouth of the cave, digging through the snow. The futile struggle of Little Sister's pups, fighting off the attack of the mountain lion, incensed her.

The lion must have killed the pups while Little Sister hunted. Coming back and finding the babies gone must have broken her heart. Summer Sky ached for her friend.

"Such a brave girl for all you've gone through. And then had enough heart to save my life that day." Summer Sky wiped her tears in Little Sister's fur and hugged her closer.

"Now you have us as your family. Come on, let's leave this sad place." Summer Sky turned away from the painful scene and walked away. Little Sister followed with a lowered head.

Entering the meadow again but with a different point of view, Summer Sky could see what the wolf had seen on that day. The girl she had howled with and danced with when they both had wanted the rabbit threatening to kill something else. The monster who had killed her babies had the girl down, crouching, prepared for attack. Physical pain gripped her chest with the weight of it all.

"This is not a good place anymore. Not until new snow covers the evidence. Lord, we walk through the valley of the shadow of death, and I know you are with us." Summer Sky reached down a hand and scratched Little Sister between the ears. Little Sister looked up then leaned against her leg. Yes, Summer Sky had no mother and Little Sister had no children. She found comfort in her new friend's presence and hoped the wolf would find comfort with her as well.

Summer Sky whistled for the horses that had wandered off near the edge of the field. Leaving this place, her only thought. The clouds had moved in, and the beautiful winter sunshine had changed. Her light heart from that morning had changed along with the weather.

Grief renewed, she walked beside Little Sister and led her family home, not concerned by the narrowness of the ledge.

*　*　*

Summer Sky set out that afternoon, turning sadness into joy for all her creature friends. Once they had reached camp, she built a fire in the outside pit and called the horses. She brushed their thick winter coats, giving them a good scratch all over their backs. She brushed the twigs and burrs out of their tails and manes. She braided and decorated Wind with feathers. On Sunshine, she braided beads and feathers into her mane and tail.

When she had finished, the daylight lessened, and dusk fell. Summer Sky dreaded removing Little Sister's stitches. She disliked tricking the wolf with sleep medicine now that she had gained her trust.

She sat beside Little Sister and watched the colors in the sky change.

"It's time, you know." Summer Sky ran her hand along the stitches. Little Sister looked over her shoulder then back at Summer Sky. They stared at each other for a time, then Summer Sky stood and went into the tipi. Little Sister followed, trusting her as if she understood her words.

Summer Sky held the door open for her friend. She latched the flap and reached her workbench; Little Sister had settled on her blanket near the fireplace. Once the meat had dried, she'd built a cache under the workbench. She reached into the cache and brought out several strips, dropped them into her skillet, then poured warm water from her kettle over the meat pieces. She added her last potato, noting she had used up the flour and had only a weeks' worth of oats left. Not even enough for a batch of oatcakes. She must find more food and soon.

Little Sister licked her face when she bent over her and

stirred the contents in the skillet. Summer Sky pushed her away with a laugh and wiped the slobber off her cheek with her forearm.

"Sweet girl, I promise, I won't hurt you." The wolf sniffed the steam coming from the skillet. Summer Sky searched for the chamomile and valerian root tincture while she chewed on a strip of meat she had fished out of the pot. She waited until the broth had thickened before spooning the tincture over the meat then she stirred and took it off the coals. She poured the mixture into a bowl and laid it beside the wolf.

Feeding the wolf had become one of their favorite pastimes. For some reason, Little Sister wouldn't eat until Summer Sky had finished her food. This time she pretended she had finished. Since Little Sister had depended on Summer Sky for her meals, it had become their ritual. From her medicine bag, Summer Sky pulled the tools she needed for clipping and pulling the stitches. The wolf enjoyed her supper.

She watched the wolf for signs the tincture had succeeded in making her sleepy. Little Sister curled up by the fire with a sigh. Summer Sky smiled at the mound of fur she had fallen in love with. Then, her practical side kicking in, she placed the tiny scissors and tweezers on the hearth of her fireplace where she had the best light for removing the sutures.

CHAPTER TWENTY-THREE

Summer Sky sat up as the wind pressed against the side of her tipi, flipping the smoke hole flap like a thimbleberry leaf in a summer breeze. Sun streamed down into the tipi for the first time in days, and she couldn't see her breath in the morning air. A chinook wind must have converged on her camp in the middle of the night. The air still had a nip to it, chilly enough she pulled her sleeping fur about her shoulders. She scooped coals together from last night's fire and piled sticks then large twigs and flames swelled. She placed her tea kettle on the fledgling fire and prepared her huckleberry leaf tea.

While Summer Sky waited for boiling water, she counted the days and weeks and months since she had taken up residence in her valley. With her knife she carved another day on her counting stick. Almost twelve weeks since she left her childhood village. She counted the weeks since the mountain lion attack, ten weeks. She and Little Sister had finished off the meat a week ago and the cache had sat empty since. Despite it not being her favorite, she still noticed the lion meat's absence with sharp awareness. And how many failures had she had with trapping or hunting since that day? She couldn't think about that.

She pulled her food bag toward her and counted enough oats for herself which may last five days. If she shared it with her friends, the food would last a day and a half. Already she had allowed herself one meal of oats. Her foraging had not brought much and nothing for the wolf. She had boiled bark and leathery mushrooms cut from dead trees. But still a handful of mushrooms couldn't sustain her through the remainder of the winter. The last time she bathed she had noticed her hips stood out from her skin at a strange and sharp angle. Her plight frightened her.

With a stretch and a yawn, Little Sister came to her side for a good morning greeting and an expectant sniff at the food bag the wolf had learned to depend on. For a long moment Summer Sky stared at her friend.

"Our food's almost gone, Little Sister. You may survive by eating once every couple of weeks, but I will need more than that." The wolf leaned against her, and Summer Sky buried her face in the soft fur around her friend's neck. The comforting presence of the animal could not stave off the fear of hunger.

What could she do?

"Lord, you provide for my every need. Your Word has taught me that you are with me in every trial. I trust in you." Little Sister whined at the door. She continued with her petition for God in her heart as she let the wolf out.

"Perhaps, Lord, you will provide through Little Sister today." With a renewed determination, Summer Sky continued with her evaluation of the situation.

"Maybe we will both have success. Hopefully, Little Sister has gone out hunting and so will I. We can't come back empty every time." Summer Sky measured a hand full of oats and dropped them into her skillet then poured hot water from her kettle over them. She stirred and counted off her other options.

"There must be food somewhere. My uncle's village north maybe." But she wouldn't take the chance, he might insist she stay.

As she ate her oatmeal in small bites, making it last longer, her thoughts listed her options, working for food, begging, and even stealing. But all that entailed leaving her home. She avoided the idea of stealing. She prayed she would never do such a thing. Fear and anxiety pressed against her chest and only subsided when she decided she would leave her sanctuary for a trip into the town she had seen in the bend of the river.

Perhaps the people there were kind, and she could trade her time for food. She could sew or clean or even cook for someone. But first, she must check her traps and maybe shoot something. With the last bite of oats still in her mouth she dressed for a day outside hunting, trapping, foraging, and praying for guidance.

*   *   *

Summer Sky calculated the round trip as taking half the time without the weighted down travois. Despite the weightlessness of riding bareback with just a food bag and her travel satchel draped over Wind's shoulders, it took the entire day before she saw the village nestled in the snow in the river valley. Thanking God, she had found it on her side of the river.

She reached the small town by twilight. Much too late to knock on the door and ask for food. Her pride swelled, shaming her. Her hunger played tricks on her mind. Of course, she should ask for food. But fear paid a visit too, reminding her of the mean people in her past.

Summer Sky peered through the trees at the first house she came across. It lay at a distance from the half dozen chimneys she had counted from a clearing above the town. Her gratitude filled her because a thick stand of trees separated the house from the rest of the town. The long day of traveling to the river town built a strong hunger that gnawed at her insides which strengthened her resolve that she had no other option. She would take what she needed. Steeling her nerves, she took several deep breaths before stepping from the cover of the forest.

"Wind, you and Little Sister stay here." She patted Wind on the neck and gave the wolf the signal for "stay".

"God, please show me now if this is what I must do. Please keep us safe and guide my path. If this is against your will, Lord, stop me."

She studied the yard a bit longer waiting for a word or sign from the Lord. The big barn across the yard had a chicken coop leaning against it. She could grab a few eggs and hoped they wouldn't miss them. Her insides sickened by the idea of stealing from hard working folk, but she could repay them with nature's remedies once she replenished her stock over the summer.

"Lord, I know in Proverbs Chapter Six you warn about stealing. And, yes, I will repay their kindness even if it takes me all summer. Maybe they have left some wheat for me on the edge of their field as in the book of Ruth."

Just as she took her first tentative steps a light in the house's window flickered as someone lit a candle inside. Summer Sky's instincts kicked in. She ducked behind a post in the corral fence, worried someone would see her. Then, she realized the window had a cloth cover that filtered the candle's glow. The light came through, but she saw no movement. She let out her held breath in a rush so loud she jumped. Her nerves skittered around inside like a drop of water on a hot skillet.

"Not every day I rob someone of their hard-earned food. Forgive me, Lord," Summer Sky whispered.

She crept across the darkened dirt road and into the yard, listening for movement in the barn or the house. She set out toward the barn then noticed a strange door built on a slight hill on one side of the house. The door seemed laid out on the ground but studying it closer, she could see it had a frame around it. It reminded her of a giant cache, big enough for a person to walk into. The location of the giant cache so near the house had gotten her heart hammering against her ribs.

Summer Sky thought for a moment that she had lost her mind for the risk she took. Riskier than the chicken coop, but she must try, or she would starve. A few eggs wouldn't sustain her until winter let go of its icy grip of the land and spring arrived.

She slipped through the pine rungs of the corral fence and hid behind the barn. Peeking around the corner, she studied the house again. She heard no cooking sounds and only a small line of smoke from the chimney confirmed supper had long passed. She had hoped whoever lived there rose early and would head for bed soon.

Taking a chance, she ran toward the cellar door and pulled it open. The hinges creaked and she stopped, not breathing, then slid inside when she didn't hear anyone coming after her. But once she let the door back down, blocking the alpenglow from outside, complete darkness engulfed her. Groping for something to prop the door open, her fingers traced a shelf and found a candle and tinder box. When she struck the flint on the rough surface of the box, it lit the room sending sparks onto the tinder and a small flame ignited. She lit the candle from the shelf.

Summer Sky looked at the cellar and marveled at the amount of food in it. Her mouth watered. Rows of food preserved in jars filled her circle of light, peaches, pears, pickles, beans, beets, cherries, and berries. Across from the fruit and vegetable jars sat smaller jars of preserved meat, red meats, pink meats, white meats, and sacks of potatoes sat on the floor under the shelves. A pile of burlap bags sat on a lower shelf above the potatoes. Summer Sky snagged one and filled it with carrots, potatoes, onions, and turnips. Then she placed a jar of peaches in the middle of the produce for protection.

Guilt gnawed at her middle, but not as strong as her hunger. She grabbed another potato and bit into it raw, dirt and all. This just nagged her deprived body into a rage, and she opened a jar of peaches, drank down the sweet nectar then slipped each quarter slice into her mouth one at a time. She set the empty jar on the shelf then thought better of it and placed it in the sack as well. The empty jar would alert the owners she had robbed them.

Further in the back of the cache, she found sausages hung from lines strung across the two rows of shelves on each wall. She took the smallest string of them and slipped it into the sack. Then, she saw what she hoped she would find. Sacks of oats and flour on the shelves across from the rows of glass jars. She placed a sack of oats and one of cornmeal inside the burlap bag and gauged its weight. She could carry it over one shoulder and the bag of flour under her arm.

She placed the food packages on the top stair and returned for the candle. Setting the tinder box just as she had found it, the candle beside it. The darkness complete, she lifted the door with her back and slipped the bags out, one by one, then followed them into the dark night.

She walked as fast as she could across the yard with her bundles of food and had almost reached the corner of the barn when the side door opened. A man stepped out with two buckets of steaming milk in each arm. White foam glistened in the light of a lantern. The light fell on Summer Sky's face as she stood motionless, not fifteen feet from the stranger.

His eyes focused on her, and she set down the packages. She hoped her sad expression conveyed the apology in her heart. She ran but only got a few steps before the man hollered at her.

"Wait, don't run off without your food."

That confused her. His food, not hers.

She looked over her shoulder, and she saw he had set the milk buckets down near the sacks she had dropped. He opened the burlap bag, then fished the empty peach jar out of the sack, took the lid off, filled it with fresh warm milk, then tightened the lid. He set it back into the sack and lifted it toward her.

What should she do? Should she break the silence and thank him, showing him, that she spoke English? No, she would keep that secret.

He didn't say another word as she stood at a distance and watched. He set the bag back down, lifted his milk buckets and proceeded toward the house, whistling.

Could he have gone inside for his gun? And if she touched the sacks, would he shoot her from the window? Her stomach tightened; she might lose what she had eaten in the cellar. Leaving that food would cost her, her health or even her life. She must take her chances.

She sprinted for the sacks. In one swift movement she had snagged them both, made it around the corner of the barn at a full run and into the woods. After stuffing the bags into the two pouches across Wind's shoulders, she leapt onto his back. At a brisk pace, they headed back up the mountain just as the moon slipped over the eastern trees and lit their way home.

CHAPTER TWENTY-FOUR

Summer Sky dozed on the back of her beloved friend. She trusted Wind and Little Sister would get her home safely. During her lucid moments throughout the night, she puzzled through the reaction of the man pouring milk into the empty peach jar and handing her the food bag.

"Generous? That must be so, but why? The bags in my hands would have convicted me, enough for the Sherriff for certain. No anger, just generosity. What does that mean?" Summer Sky mumbled and watched her frosted breath waft in front of her and dissipate.

The farmer's confusing kindness made her uncomfortable. As far back as she could remember, most people had treated her with anything but kindness. Most of her mother's people showed acceptance, but not the children. They used Summer Sky's differences as a weapon.

She expected her mother's love and kindness, but not from a stranger, from whom she had stolen. Her head hurt. She pondered over the workings of that man's mind.

Wind stopped his swaying walk, and Summer Sky looked around. They had made it home. During the journey back, she had made note of the moon which crossed the dark sky, and now hovered over the western horizon. They had traveled many miles for this food, almost a full day and night.

Exhausted, she slid off Wind's back, and her legs buckled, landing her on her knees. Cold and numb from a lack of circulation, she pulled herself up. She slipped her stash of food down and dragged it into the tipi, a warm fire and sleep her priority.

But the milk drew her attention first, and then, the rest of the food. Once she had the fire blazing, she set the bags on her workbench and sorted the goods. The milk jar had settled on the bottom with the peaches, and she said a prayer of thanks they hadn't clanked together and broken.

She poured a drizzle of creamy milk into her cup then set the water heating for tea. Impatient for the boiling water, she took a sip from the jar and the fresh cold milk trailed a delicious tingle through her body. What a special treat, she couldn't recall how long it had been since she'd had milk.

Summer Sky took her chamomile tea with milk and crawled into bed. Setting her tea down, she lit the lamp on her nightstand and pulled her father's bible into her lap. Little Sister followed her for a good scratch then plopped down as near as she could.

She smiled at the thought she'd had during the wolf's convalescence, that someday she would say goodbye once Little Sister had healed. However, the wolf seemed happy with Summer Sky. Flipping through the bible, she read through some Psalms since her fatigue kept her from diving in too deep. Psalm 32 caught her eye.

"Blessed are the ones whose transgressions are forgiven, whose sins are covered. Blessed is the one whose sin the Lord does not count against him and in whose Spirit, there is no deceit." Summer Sky scrunched up her eyebrows. "Lord, I'm so sorry for stealing. My mother taught me better than that. I won't do it again. I will trust you for my provision. Perhaps if I go back, they will forgive me and trade with me. I could work for them and pay off what I took. Thank you for forgiving me. Good night, Lord, I love you."

As the chamomile tea took effect, and Summer Sky's eyes drooped, the sun rose on the eastern horizon sending pink rays across the open smoke hole flap. She closed her father's bible, the words written by King David brought correction and comfort. She drifted off with a sigh.

∗   ∗   ∗

Summer Sky dreamt about the man's kindness. The smile on his face made his eyes dance. His warmth and love spilled from him through his laughter.

She opened her eyes and looked out the smoke hole, gauging the time as mid-afternoon.

Rolling over, she looked for Little Sister then noticed the bottom toggle of the door flap pulled from its eye, leaving a small opening. Clever girl, opening the door herself. Summer Sky must have slept deep, she hadn't heard her whining. Her stomach growled notifying her she hadn't eaten since the peaches and raw potato in the cellar. She dressed and grabbed everything she needed for outside cooking. At the last minute she grabbed her hairbrush and her father's bible.

Blue sky and the warmth of sunshine on her face welcomed her. She laughed at her sleepy friend. Little Sister opened one eye in greeting as she snoozed in the sun on a blanket. Then she saw it, the gift of another rabbit lying beside the cold firepit.

"Thank you, Lord, I appreciate your blessings beyond measure. And thank you Little Sister for the rabbit." Summer Sky sunk onto her knees and hugged the wolf until she squirmed. With a laugh and another squeeze, she let go and kneeled by the firepit.

After building a good hot fire, she sliced potatoes and sausage into her skillet with some fat and then prepared the rabbit for her oven. She kept adding more wood and scooping embers toward the side with a green branch, building enough for roasting the rabbit. It would slow roast for a few hours until it tendered and fell off the bones.

As she ate the sausage and her first fried potato in weeks, she flipped through her bible. She searched for a story that had played in her mind since she awakened. The story of feeding the poor. She searched in the Old Testament, and she hadn't read that part of the bible as much as she had the New Testament.

The book of Ruth stood out as she fanned through and stopped. She read through the short story with shock and admiration for the woman who would show her loyalty and trust. Ruth obeyed and found a faith in God that blessed nations. Ruth and her mother-in-law had nothing, not even food. Ruth went out and gleaned wheat and barley from the outside of the fields. Generous farmers would leave enough grain on the edges for the poor. Boaz had become Ruth and Naomi's kinsman redeemer and brought them both into his family.

"There is no shame in being poor or hungry. The shame comes from when I didn't ask but just took. I believe if I had knocked on the door and asked, they would have given me what I needed. I think that's what the farmer showed me when he filled the peach jar with milk. Is that what I must learn, Lord?"

Her heart filled with gratitude for the farmer, for Little Sister, for Wind, and most of all for God who had carried her through every challenging thing she had faced. God had forgiven her for so much.

She went inside and got a jar for the cream. Making butter took time, so she grabbed a few more things. The oats, and some flour from the workbench. She hadn't put everything away from her journey. In a bowl, she mixed the ingredients with some lard from her supply. Instead of forming cakes, she scooped a bit out with a spoon and dropped it into her hot skillet, smashing it down with the spoon.

She watched the snow melt in the sun and shrink away from the inlet of the little lake as she braided her long silky hair. Could spring be on its way? Her heart content with her life, she sat near Little Sister still snoozing and smelled the oatcakes baking in her skillet.

"Lord, thank you for your forgiveness. I will not steal again. I will trust you for my every need." Summer Sky raised her face toward the heavens in thanksgiving.

"You are forgiven. Do not fear for what you will eat. I will provide for you." She heard a quiet voice in her soul.

She seldom heard God's voice; and it overwhelmed her as her throat thickened with emotion that the God of the universe should love her enough to sustain her.

"Did you provide that farm for me, Lord?" He may have guided her, but Summer Sky's pride had kept her from knocking on the door. And maybe even the fear of another person rejecting her. She waited for a response, but she heard nothing. Yet a flood of peace washed over her, the silence itself an answer.

CHAPTER TWENTY-FIVE

Summer Sky stepped out of her tipi, Little Sister followed her with a yawn and a stretch. Hot tea warmed her hands and her face as she breathed in the steam with relish. She dreamed of peppermint and rosehips, both long gone until spring. She had no hope of finding more this far into the winter season.

A hint of light brightened the eastern horizon. She watched in awe, as she had done with every sunrise and sunset, the beams of light planted pink and yellow streaks across the sky, fanning out into the darkness. Snow had fallen through the night and blanketed her trails with a new, clean white cover that brought a thrill of happiness.

"Lord, thank you for your beautiful painting this morning."

Smiling, she turned and faced the day. She looked around and noticed the woodpile needed replenishing and since an odor billowed out of her coat with every movement, she should bathe. She would need plenty of wood for washing herself and her clothes. The fear she experienced at the farm had left its stench on her.

She snagged the empty kettle off the iron arm that suspended it over the outdoor fire pit and slogged through the fluffy powder toward the spring. The snow-covered hills in her valley thrilled her, they looked clean and brand new. Today, she focused on healing and praising.

Little Sister trotted behind her toward the spring. After lapping up her fill, she darted into the bushes. Maybe the wolf would bring a rabbit home for supper.

Summer Sky watched the pink and yellow of the sunrise

change, tinting the clouds deep red and lavender as the sun crested the mountains in the east. Color in the clouds tolled a warning of a storm coming, she had known this all her life. She resigned herself for a day inside.

While her bath water heated, she took her hatchet into the forest for wood. After cutting and dragging several small, dead trees into her campsite, she chopped until she had no strength left in her arms, all the while watching the sky.

The clouds had built a dark bank over the cliff, north of her tipi. As she brought in the wood, the storm brewed. Summer Sky filled her indoor and outdoor kettles and brought them inside. She would wait out whatever may come, safe and warm.

She hauled her large washing pan near the fire and waited for the water to warm. Taking a clean cotton under dress and a wool skirt from her mother's clothing chest, she laid them aside on her sleeping platform. A quiet afternoon, snuggled in her warm home wearing her mother's things would cheer her up. She had never liked storms; the unpredictable nature of the weather heightened the unease twisting in her belly.

After brushing her long hair, she kneeled in front of the basin, flipped her hair over her head and poured cups of warm water over it. She grabbed the bar of soap her mother and her best friend Merri had made with specks of fragrant lavender suspended in the bar. She lathered her hair and rinsed, pouring water from the kettle over her head and into her wash basin. Then with a soft cloth, she washed the rest of her, including behind her ears, recalling her mother's teachings with a smile. She washed her feet and her clothes at the same time, stomping and swishing the water around in her wash tub.

As she dressed and put on her fur lined slippers that reached her knees, her clothes soaked. Then she rolled up her sleeves, wrung out her laundry and draped each piece on a line she had strung across the tipi. The warmth of a blazing fire and the drying garments filled the air with lavender scented moisture.

On her cattail woven mat, she brushed the tangles out of

her damp hair and braided it in front of the fire. As she tied off her second braid, the door flap pushed in, and Little Sister stepped inside. The animal huffed, out of breath, as if she had run a long way home.

"There you are. I worried you were caught in the storm."

Little Sister plopped down on her mat near the fire and sighed.

"What have you been doing all day?" Summer Sky hadn't expected a response but reached over and petted her friend on the scruff of her neck. She noticed Little Sister's hair had mats of snow dripping from the warmth of the fire. She must have traveled quite a distance to have her belly and legs covered in clots of snow.

"Poor thing. You're soaked." Summer Sky pulled a dry towel off the line and rubbed her friend down. Once she reached Little Sister's healing wound, the wolf flinched and grabbed the flannel cloth with her teeth and pulled. They played tug-of-war for a bit then the wolf jumped up with a yip and a dance as she evaded Summer Sky's toweling. With laughter, Summer Sky plopped down on a mat in front of the fire. Little Sister crawled over and placed her head in Summer Sky's lap with a sigh.

Their bond had deepened as the winter days had passed. While Little Sister snored beside her, Summer Sky carved another day on her counting stick. With each notch she counted seven then made that seventh longer, representing a week. She counted back, determining the days and weeks since her long journey had begun. The weeks added up. Sixteen weeks, mid-March with spring just days away. But would spring come this far up in the mountains so soon? In the sunny spots around meadows, she may find fresh greens, but the snow must melt first.

The wind blasted and pushed in the door flap where she had left it open for Little Sister. Walking toward the door, she noticed snow blowing in. She poked her head out and noted the storm had reached them. She had trouble gauging the time, the sky broiled with dark clouds that dumped their snow upon the earth, nurturing and blanketing her home with the needed moisture that would fill the rivers and streams and feed the plants, fish, and animals as well as the people.

"Thank you, Lord, for your provision. Heal our hearts and our land from the terrible sickness." Summer Sky secured the door flap and noticed Little Sister watching her.

"I bet you're hungry after your adventure today. So am I." Summer Sky gathered what she needed from the work bench and the cache. She pulled out the last sausage, two potatoes, an onion, and three strips of dried meat. She grabbed salt, wild fennel, wild garlic, butter, and flour and made a meaty stew she thought Little Sister would enjoy.

The wind howled through the trees and the smoke hole as the stew bubbled. Little Sister watched the steam float through the air from the skillet and licked away the slobber accumulating on her lips in anticipation.

Summer Sky served two bowls and sat Little Sister's on the hearth until it cooled. The wolf would not eat until Summer Sky had finished. She blew on a hot spoonful of stew and ate too fast, burning her mouth. She slowed down despite the staring wolf near her.

With her last bite in her mouth, she gauged the temperature of Little Sister's portion, and plopped the wolf's bowl onto the tipi floor. While the wolf ate, Summer Sky slipped her parka over her head. She needed more wood in case the storm lasted longer than expected. The wolf followed her out.

"You finished already?" Summer Sky closed the door flap and stepped into a different world. Instead of the brightness of mid-afternoon that she had expected, the darkened sky seemed more like that of sunset. The dark clouds hung low, and the snow had gathered thick over the pile of wood. The wind blew her hood off her head, and she fastened it with the rawhide ties under her chin. The deep snow surprised her. Summer Sky studied the clouds again guessing they had a lot more snow left in them.

She moved toward the side of the tipi examining the

smoke hole in the dim light. Snowflakes swirled around her in an unhelpful way. Her only option in this situation, protect the flap. She must secure it part way yet leave it open enough for the escaping smoke. Once done, she slogged through the snow, concentrating on the trail in the dim light. She filled her kettle for her night tea and as she stood, she heard a growl from Little Sister behind her.

Summer Sky stepped away from the spring thinking another animal had chosen that moment for his evening drink, giving whatever animal some space. Little Sister pushed past her and growled again, standing her ground while guarding Summer Sky. Summer Sky backed up a couple steps on shaking legs. Little Sister backed up as well, still head down and growling, showing her terrifying teeth.

As they reached the tipi, she fumbled with the flap, her hands shaking. Her eyes darted over the area as her heartbeat slammed against her ribs. The snow had limited her view, giving Summer Sky goose bumps. The hairs on the back of her neck stood in anticipation of an attack. She had no idea what menace lurked just inside the tree line on the other side of the spring, the darkness of the afternoon and the shadows between the trees kept her from seeing. Not knowing what lurked inside the forest seemed far worse than meeting the enemy face-to-face. She chided herself again for being unprepared and not arming herself.

She imagined Little Sister had scared off the threat, her fierce friend a formidable challenger. Safe in the tipi with the door flap firmly closed, she stoked the fire and put on a full kettle of water. She watched as Little Sister sat staring at the door as if waiting for company.

Summer Sky hoped not.

CHAPTER TWENTY-SIX

The wind blew throughout the night. At times, Summer Sky heard cracking and crashing as branches broke. She imagined them bouncing off trees on their way down, disappearing in the powder of the snow below.

Dim light filtering through the narrow gap of the smoke hole told her morning had arrived. However, the wind still howled and had blown fine snow between the cracks around the door flap, building tiny drifts inside the tipi. Summer Sky burrowed into her furs, warming her chilled nose and cheeks. The temperature had dropped through the night, the air inside her tipi bitter cold. She slipped off her sleeping mat, crawling toward the fireplace still wrapped in her warm furs. She built a fire and heated water for tea.

Little Sister whined as she paced. Summer Sky slipped into her warm winter clothing and joined her at the door flap. She pulled the toggles out of their holes and pushed but it wouldn't open. She pushed on the uppermost part of the door, and it gave some. A drift must have built against the side of her tipi, blocking off their exit. She pushed harder, but still, it wouldn't budge. She pulled the flap inward a bit and peeked at the wall of snow. At the top she could see light filtering through. Little Sister panted at the door as if wondering about the hold up. Summer Sky understood her friend's plight and experienced the same importance.

She moved alongside her workbench where she kept her tools and grabbed her father's metal shovel. She dumped the blankets out of her mother's storage trunk onto the bed and dragged the trunk over the floor, the largest container she had for that much snow. Shovel full by shovel full, Summer Sky dug them out of the tipi. It took quite a bit of time before she had the door cleared far enough for Little Sister's departure.

Summer Sky climbed out after the wolf, dragging the trunk behind her through the narrow hole. She dumped it on the side of her tipi and went back for more. The treetops swayed, shaking free the light crystals of accumulated snow into the air. When the sun peeked from behind the racing clouds, it bounced off the snow, blinding her.

The clouds whisked past, roiling. Still shoveling the snow from the path, she made her way toward her buried outdoor firepit. The bitter wind bit at her, stinging the exposed skin across her face. She put her arm over her mouth and cheeks, stopping the burning onslaught as she looked through the cold-induced tears that streamed from her eyes. It seemed she must spend another day inside.

Once she had cleared the door of snow, she brought the trunk back inside and placed it near the fire. Then, grabbing her snowshoes and shrugging her bow and quiver over each shoulder, she headed for the spring. She wouldn't see any tracks because of the new snow, but she would stay vigilant. Searching across the expanse of white, she wondered where her protector had gone.

She made her way toward the spring, but the water had frozen, silent in the vast white. The wind had piled snow against the mound where the beavers had built their home. Her now drifted-in trail no longer existed. The storm had whitewashed the world around her, a pristine clean, as if she walked through a dream world. The trees stood like ghosts. An eerie whistling caused a shiver as the wind rushed through the bare branches of the aspens on the other side of the lake.

As Summer Sky studied her surroundings, she scouted the best place for clean snow and plowed through the drifts toward the tipi. She filled the large kettle and brought it inside, placing it on the fire. Then, she poured a bit of warm water into the snow from the little kettle she used for tea. With her shovel in her hand, she forced herself outside again. She must dig out her wood pile. She brought several armfuls inside, stacking them against the wall. Still, the wind howled through the trees, throwing snow down through the smoke hole.

Settling in for the time being, she sipped on warm tea curled up in a blanket by the fire.

"Thank you, Lord, for the weather that puts my work on hold. May today be as though it's a sabbath reprieve." Holding her father's bible against her chest she contemplated what she should read, then opened the bible, flipping to the book of James.

"Count it all joy when you fall into various trials, knowing that the testing of your faith produces patience." Summer Sky read aloud the words which slipped into her heart like balm over a wound. Count it all joy. Words so foreign, yet she yearned for the promise. The promise of joy in patience. For the moment, she practiced patience while waiting out the windstorm, which at intervals, fluttered at the smoke hole flap.

She hadn't seen the horses for a few days and worried about them with the unknown predator in their sanctuary. However, they looked out for each other, and she had enough trouble taking care of herself. Staying on guard had become her daily chore. She missed the days when the entire village kept everyone safe. At least, she had Little Sister, but for how long? Soon, Little Sister might want a new family of her own. Could that howl they had heard come from a male wolf looking for a mate?

The thought saddened and gladdened Summer Sky at the same time. Happy for her friend but dreading letting her go. She had enjoyed her company through the long, lonely nights, and it eased the grief of missing her mother.

She set her bible on the crate beside her bed and settled in front of the fireplace stirring cornmeal bubbling in the skillet. She heard scratching at the door flap and opened the door for Little Sister.

"There you are. You look a fright." Summer Sky grabbed a towel just as Little Sister shook. She held it up, catching the matted slush as it splattered everything in sight. Laughing, she lunged for the wolf guessing it would become a game. Evading the toweling Summer Sky intended, Little Sister jumped and twisted in midair, landing with the corner of the cloth in her mouth. With a flick of her head, she pulled it out of Summer Sky's hands.

"You little rascal. Give that back, you thief." Laughing louder, she lunged for her friend again, but this time ended up face down. She rolled onto the cattail mat in front of the fireplace and got a face full of an energetic licking tongue.

"Stop, stop. I give, you win." With a sigh and out of breath from laughing so hard, she plopped down and stirred her meal. While eating her hot cereal, she wondered at the antics of her friend who laid by the fire licking her wet fur. She could tell Little Sister had run for a good distance, gauging by the clumps of snow frozen to her belly and legs again. She must have regained her stamina, traveling further from their home than she had in the past. Summer Sky could sense their time growing shorter. The days had become longer; the arc of the sun through the sky pushed higher as spring drew near.

Resolved, Summer Sky focused on each day with Little Sister as a gift. She watched her friend, determined to enjoy every moment.

In the afternoon, she noticed a stillness and hoped it meant the storm had passed. Peeking through the half-opened door flap, her heart filled with hope. The clouds had skittered away, and the sun had come out with the easing of the wind. The afternoon sparkled in the crisp air.

"Come on my friend, let's find the horses." She scratched the top of Little Sister's head as she passed her and prepared for the rest of the day outside.

The weather had turned lovely. With her snowshoes on, her weapons slung over each shoulder and her food bag resting on her hip with oat cakes, she headed toward the cliff, hoping the horses had found safety in their cave from the storm. Summer Sky whistled, wondering if the horses would join them in the meadow above as she headed in the direction of the trail. She had missed them.

Despite her snowshoes, she sunk in the dust-like snow. The trip up the trail, through the drifts, slowed her down and winded her by the time she reached the cave. The sunlight angled its light up the inner wall of one side, but she found it empty. Disappointed and frightened for the horses, she continued toward the top of the cliff into the fated meadow where she had taken down her first kill. Her only kill so far.

She whistled again, and she heard a whinny come from the forest beyond. Then, Sunshine and Wind broke out of the trees. Plowing through the snow they ran toward Summer Sky with a white cloud of snow billowing around them in a halo of rainbow-colored sparkles. The sun glinted off each tiny star-like flake.

Their abrupt stop showered Summer Sky with ice cold droplets that stung her cheeks. It didn't matter, happiness filled her seeing the two unharmed. She hoped the menacing animal had moved on. Untying her snowshoes and sticking them upright in the snow, marking their location, she grabbed a fist of Wind's mane and swung herself onto his back.

With a war cry, Summer Sky urged Wind into a run and relished a tingling sensation as her hood flew off and the snow floated around them in the sunshine, a cocoon of fractured light so beautiful it took her breath away.

They ran together as one in a world all their own around the meadow. Out of the corner of her eye she saw a streak of grey heading in her direction. Wind saw it too and he stopped with a sudden binding of all his muscles, Summer Sky flew over his head and landed in a heap. Buried in the deep snow face down, she heard a tussle near her, then growling and snorting. It sounded like an animal had attacked Wind.

Frantic, she struggled to get her footing. Swiping melting snow from her eyes and collar she recognized Little Sister in a fighting stance. Wind, with wild eyes, stomped and would charge the wolf at any moment.

"Stop," She hollered over the ruckus of the argument between her two friends. She whistled for attention, and they both looked at her with wide eyes.

In a rush of what seemed like worry, the animals sped over. Little Sister jumped up putting her paws on Summer Sky's shoulders and licked the snow off her face. Still unsteady from the fall, she toppled back from the animal's weight. The argument erupted again as each friend vied for her attention.

"You two stop, this minute. You know I love you both. Now stop." Her firm voice brought them toward her with heads bowed in obedience. She reached out, calming their nervous excitement, and a pain shot up her left arm. She hadn't noticed until that moment; she must have injured herself when she flew off Wind's back.

She pulled her arm tight against her chest with her right hand and hoped it wasn't serious. The fun over, she shoved her way through the deep snow toward her snowshoes and headed back down the path with the animals following behind. Her official ruling, she labeled the cliff meadow dangerous.

CHAPTER TWENTY-SEVEN

Summer Sky worked her parka over her head with a hiss through her teeth at the pain in her arm. She stoked the fire, then lit the lamp on her nightstand with one-handed awkwardness. She set the lamp on her workbench. Her arm throbbed as she held it against her body. Pulling the sleeve up, she hissed again. Bruising had spread across her wrist and palm.

"Dear God, please tell me it's not broken. Please, strengthen it with your healing power. In Jesus' name." Summer Sky pulled it back into a comforting cradle against her chest as her vision blurred with unshed tears. She searched her memory and sorted through the jars of dried medicinal plants and bottles of tinctures. Her mother had used a special blend of herbs that created a potent pain reliever, stronger than willow bark tea.

She needed something external for a poultice that could reduce swelling, but for now she grabbed a bowl, went outside, and filled it with snow. She put it in an empty flour sack and tied the pack as best she could around her throbbing wrist using her right hand and her teeth.

With the cold pack freezing the ache, she searched the shelves for remedies. The pain in her wrist and the months of solitude dissolved. She stood in front of the workbench as if her mother stood beside her. She could even hear her mother's teaching voice.

"You must be careful with this combination. If you get the amounts wrong the remedy will be too strong in the pain relieving and weak in the calming and numbing effects. One part Corydalis, two parts Snap Dragon Skullcap, and five parts Selfheal. Stuff it all in the jar. Yes, like that. Now mix three parts alcohol with one part water."

"Like this, Mama?" Summer Sky could almost smell the strong distilled liquid her mother used for her tinctures.

"Well done, now pour it over the chopped Medicinals in the jar. Make sure you cover all the herbs. Seal the jar and set it in the back. I leave it for a few weeks. After the steeping is over, you strain the herbs then it will be ready. You can even use the leftovers as a poultice."

"How much do I give my patient?" Summer Sky asked with a teasing smile. Water Lily laughed at the smirk on her daughter's face.

"Your patient only needs a half teaspoon if you don't have a dropper or five drops from the glass tube. Dribble it under the tongue. Make sure your patient holds it there for a count of twenty then swallow. That will do the trick."

The vision of her mother dissolved, and the loss seemed less than in the past.

"Mother, you have taught me so much." She hoped one day she would use all her knowledge for the benefit of others the way her mother had.

"Now, I must make it from memory. My patient is myself this time." Summer Sky read the labels tied around each jar, finding the right tincture. She had mixed-up the jars and baskets in the move and stacked them in a hurry. She hadn't organized them yet. Her mother had ancient wisdom from her family's healers from generations past. The years she had practiced her healing trade, she'd had no doubt about where she had placed her remedies. Summer Sky hadn't reached that level of expertise, not yet.

"Here it is." She took a hollow glass stir stick, dipped it into the tincture and placed her finger over the top end, then tilted her head back. Lifting her tongue, she dripped the bitter and tangy liquid into her mouth.

One, two, three, four, and five. She counted out the dose in her head then closed her mouth letting the stinging alcohol pool under her tongue while she put the lid back on and cleaned the stir stick. She noted the time by the daylight through the smoke hole, around mid-day. She must hurry with the poultice and splint before the medicine took effect.

She searched through the baskets that held the dried herbs for what she needed for a poultice. She set out three and kept searching.

"I don't have any snapdragon skullcap left. These will work, though." She opened each small basket and with all her fingers she took a large pinch of each and dumped them into her stone bowl.

With the pestle she smashed together the dried yarrow, corydalis and selfheal, then added hot water, making a thick paste. She scooped a portion and smeared it onto a flannel bandage she had placed on her workbench. She tried cutting the cloth with one hand but failed. She wrapped the whole bandage around her wrist even though she hated wasting cloth she couldn't replace.

"Now, what should I use for a splint?" She searched around for the right size piece of wood from her wood pile. Her swollen and throbbing wrist kept her from chopping one smaller. The medicine took effect. Her vision blurred and she couldn't concentrate.

She couldn't find what she needed, nothing she had worked. Giving up, she wrapped another bandage around her body and strapped her arm against her chest. She added more wood on the fire and crawled into bed. Her eye lids drooped, and her sleepy mind lingered over a vision of a herd of wild horses she had seen as a young child while visiting family in the Montana territory. And, like the horses, sleep rushed at her as a tangible force.

*   *   *

Sleep and strange dreams. A dream of her mother...
... "What do you mean, Mama?"
"Your journey will be hard, my love, but do not give

into despair. I taught you well. Life has taught you lessons on perseverance. Keep your strength close."

"You are frightening me with this talk. I am not strong, not without you."

"Ah, you think you are without me. Look around, my love, I am in the plants you will harvest, I am in your mind with my voice still teaching you. And I am with the Lord and so are you. You must lean on your faith, my child, my darling girl. I am sorry I must leave you again."

"Mama, please take me with you."

"I cannot, for you must survive in this world. Yes, you are too young for so much. Trust God, and do not lean on your own, childlike, understanding. Trust him. He will bring you through."

"Mama, don't go just yet."

"Trust God, my love."

Summer Sky woke in darkness and Little Sister whining at the door. The wispy fog of the dream still floated in her head.

"Mama, don't go," Summer Sky whispered, she needed her mother. She pulled the toggle out of the bottom hole of the door flap and let the wolf in. Little Sister whined and sniffed the strong poultice on her arm. The wolf circled Summer Sky as if consoling her. She squatted down, level with the wolf, and with her good hand scratched the animal behind the ear.

The pain had subsided. She sat in front of the firepit and fished around for coals. Once she had gathered enough, her stomach growled. She dropped one of her last potatoes into the hot coals, then piled kindling on cedar bark shavings. Tucking a coal into her fire starter, she blew until it flamed up. Then scooping a cup of cornmeal out of the almost empty bag, she made a paste and dropped portions of it into her hot skillet. Her mother had taught her she must always put something in her stomach before treating with more pain reliever.

While she waited for her batch of corncakes, she searched her wood pile for a splint. Hefting her hatchet, she whittled down a couple kindling pieces and wrapped them in a soft cloth. Grabbing the bowl she had soaked her injury in the night before, she threw the water outside and scooped fresh snow, preparing for another soak. She unwrapped her wrist.

Summer Sky examined the damage she had done flying off the back of Wind. A yellowish green colored bruise around the edges covered her wrist with a deep purple in the center where the wrist met the hand. She contemplated the meaning of the colors in relation to the type of injury. A bad sprain or worse, broken.

While she waited for her potato, her mouth watered, thinking about the sweet butter she had made with the cream from the farm. She had used the last of it on a potato a couple of days ago. It seemed so long since she had found that farm. With her wrist still in a bowl of snow she couldn't reach her counting stick, she guessed four weeks had passed. Spring must show itself soon.

Her cache of meat stored a couple more days of meals. She had used up the oats along with the small string of sausages. She must ask the farmer for more food. With a shudder of frustration about her lack of supplies, her survival instinct outweighed her fear of people.

Once she had eaten a couple of corncakes, she reached for the bottle of pain reliever. She dribbled a dose under her tongue and held it there for a count of twenty. She checked her potato but decided it needed more time then scooped more coals over it. The bowl of snow melted, she lifted her arm out and dried it off with a soft cloth. She spread more herbal paste into a new cloth bandage and wrapped it around her wrist. She took the other end of the bandage and wrapped it around her palm and between each finger, stabilizing the bones in her hand from moving. She placed the two splint pieces on the top and bottom of her arm and bandaged her forearm and hand, keeping the wrist from moving.

She glanced at the smoke hole and the color of the muted light that filtered in had a pink tinge. The afternoon had slipped past her. She poured hot water over tea leaves in her cup. Her movements awkward with one hand, she rose and made it outside and watched the last rays of the sun leave the cliff.

CHAPTER TWENTY-EIGHT

Summer Sky flung her travel bag with extra clothes, and her mother's moccasins in case she needed them, over Wind's back. She had packed the remaining food as well. She threw a sleeping fur around her. With a rope, she tied it over her chest, over each shoulder securing her injured arm, then knotted the rope in the front. The extra layer added warmth against the frigid morning air. Then she hooked her quiver over the saddle horn along with her bow.

She hadn't seen her mother's horse for some time now, and she worried. She hoped Sunshine had made her way out of the mountains and found the other horses. The night had stayed cold, and a fresh dusting of snow had come with it. Wolf howls had interrupted Summer Sky's sleep as Little Sister fretted and whined at the door.

She noticed Little Sister had stayed away for longer periods of time the last few days. Summer Sky assumed her friend had found a mate and spent her time searching for a new home, safe from predators. Despite Little Sister's loyalty, Summer Sky must let her go and the moment had come.

The trip toward town would distance her from her beloved wolf. Heartbreaking, but necessary for Little Sister. Summer Sky wouldn't hold her friend back. She wondered about her own future. Would she find someone who would want a confused and ugly child like her? No one wanted her.

"I don't need anyone." She set her jaw, accepting a solitary life.

"I am independent because I have always been alone, except for my mother." Independence had protected her from the mistreatment she endured from the village children.

"I would rather spend the rest of my life alone before I suffer that again."

The other children never wanted her in their games or even ordinary everyday life with them. Raven showed her compassion when the children circled her, but she would never see her again. A stab of loneliness weighed heavy in her heart when she thought of the girl who might have become her friend, but for the great sickness.

Her aloneness reminded her of Little Sister. Would the wolf find a mate that stuck around this time? Would he help bear the load of protecting Little Sister's babies? Summer Sky sent a prayer for peace in whatever God had in store for Little Sister and herself. Peace came as she struggled onto Wind's back with only one hand. Her determined heart prepared for the meeting with the farmer.

She would speak with him this time and tell him how much she regretted stealing from his family. They set out as the sun crested the mountains east of her home. She looked back at the tipi making sure she had secured the smoke hole and door flap well.

Something twisted inside her, fear. She must have heard something. The little hairs on the back of her neck prickled her skin and she shivered. She scanned the tree line. Yellow eyes stared at her from the face of the largest wolf she had ever seen. Little Sister made a yip and wagged her tail. Could she have found a mate already? Her friend paused and looked up at Summer Sky as if asking permission for a happy life for herself.

Summer Sky slid off her horse. On her knees in the new snow, she hugged her friend tight. Little Sister's fur soaked up the stream of tears that slipped down her face.

"I will miss you so much, Little Sister. But don't you worry about me. I will not forget you and imagine you with your pups playing in the forest." Her voice broke, and a sob escaped her tight throat. Little Sister whined. Summer Sky gasped for air through the weight of goodbye.

"This time you will succeed in raising your babies," she said through sniffles.

"You are loved." Summer Sky hugged her tighter, and Little Sister licked her face. Laughing and crying, Summer Sky pushed the wolf away and wiped the slobber off with her sleeve.

"Alright, enough kisses. Go on, my friend. Be happy and safe." Summer Sky pushed her friend away again and pointed toward where she had seen the wolf. "Go on."

The wolf looked at her, then turned her head toward the woods. With a happy yip and a flip in the air, Little Sister trotted away, looking back only once before stepping into the woods. Summer Sky sat in the snow already missing the comfort her friend had brought her through the grieving. Little Sister filled the void her mother had left.

But she still had Wind. He had stayed even after Sunshine had left for lower ground, perhaps searching for better grass. She pushed herself up with one mittened hand in the snow. With her splinted wrist still tied against her chest, she dusted herself off as best she could. She climbed onto her horse for the trip out of the mountains.

The snow deepened as they made their way out of the little valley. In places, Wind slogged through drifts nearing his chest which made the going more difficult. The wind kicked up and blew snow in their faces. As the day progressed, it warmed. The snow in the trees slipped off branches, plopping wet clumps of slush on them. She studied Wind's movements for any indication he needed a break. The hardship of winter in Summer Sky's valley proved itself by Wind's bony ribs which she noticed through her leggings. Her bones, too, had far less padding against the solidness of her saddle.

Slow and steady, though, Wind took everything in stride. Sure, and loyal, he put one foot in front of the other until they had reached a more manageable level of snow. Even so, the hillside remained steep and closed in. Summer Sky spied a flat spot between the trees and steered Wind in that direction. She thought it a good place for a break.

She slid off her horse. Then she heard it. The deep grumbling sound of rushing water. They stood on a snow bridge. Water thundered down the steep ravine, cold and under the snow beneath them. The spring runoff.

The hairs on the back of her neck stood up as if aware of the danger she and Wind had gotten themselves into. She took the end of the reins and gave him plenty of space, spreading the weight load over the dangerous bridge in hopes it would hold.

Summer Sky had almost reached the other side. A few more steps. But Wind had several feet before he crossed. One step. Then another. She drew Wind closer. Willed him toward safety.

Crack. The panic in Wind's eyes must have mirrored hers. She resisted the urge to pull hard on his reins. Another crack and Wind hunkered down preparing for a jump toward her. She stepped aside and the snow under her gave way.

Wind leapt to stable ground. The bridge crumbled with a roar. Her one hand gripped the reins tighter while she struggled to free her injured arm. The strength of the rushing water tore at her. Her feet searched for a foothold. She dangled there over a waterfall. Wind backed up, dragging Summer Sky with him. With every pull he slipped closer toward the edge. Her weight on his harness dragged him down. Her mittened hand slipped further on the reins.

"God, help me," She screamed. Her good hand gripped her only lifeline. Every muscle in her arm cried out for release.

Water filled her moccasins and ripped them off her feet, one by one. She took a last look at Wind as her strength spilled out of her.

"I'm sorry, my friend. Stay well." Summer Sky filled her lungs and held it. Then, she let go.

The cold shocked her. It nearly took the breath from her lungs. She kept her feet in front of her through the dark tunnel of rushing water. Her legs cushioned the brunt of each rock. The roof of snow and ice scraped her hand and face. The rushing water slammed her again and again. Into the frozen tunnel she plummeted. Searing pain flushed through her for only a moment before the frigid water numbed each injury. She couldn't hold her breath much longer.

Jesus... Jesus... Jesus. The name of her savior became her focus on repeat.

Desperate for air and survival, she struggled with the heavy fur she had made into a cape for the trip. With her numb fingers, she couldn't loosen the knot using only one hand. Her lungs screamed for air. Summer Sky attempted the knot again, but still couldn't free her injured arm. She tumbled down the ravine, under the snow and under the water.

Then, her struggle ended as she folded around a giant boulder and got stuck. The impact knocked the air from her lungs. It rushed out in a stream of bubbles that pointed her toward the surface. She held onto the rock and climbed. The current pounding against her back. She clung to hope. Free of the suffocating water, her lungs filled with a wheeze.

"HELP," she screamed again and again until her voice cracked.

She hugged the rock and searched for a way out of the grip of waves that still pulled on her. Blessed daylight proved no help as she searched in vain for an overhanging branch or log she could reach, bringing her toward shore. Her numb fingers couldn't hold onto the slippery rock much longer. Years of water rushing over the solid surface had sanded the granite smooth of even a slight crack for a better grip.

Shivering and with teeth clattering, loud in her head, she couldn't think. She saw nothing that would free her from this nightmare.

The waterlogged fur tugged at her.

"No. NO. Help" she screamed with what little strength she had left. "Help me." She inhaled great gulps of rattling breaths dreading the inevitable.

The weight of the rushing water and the fur peeled her off the life-saving rock. She inhaled another desperate breath. Summer Sky plunged back into the ice-cold water. Feet in front, she reminded herself. Pain shot up her leg as she bounced off a sharp rock. She rolled and tumbled out of control. Her lungs and her mind played tug of war. Who would win? White flashes of light exploded behind her closed eyes.

She steeled herself against the idea of losing the fight. Her body felt numb. Peace replaced the stabbing cold. The tug of water disappeared. She floated, then the current ripped her across sharp rocks. She tasted blood. Dark. Then light. Then, dark again. Confusion clouded. The water carried.

Her depleted strength and the cold had stolen her hope. She let the water take her down. Acceptance filled her as the truth dawned. She would see her mother soon. Blackness, peace, warmth. She let go.

CHAPTER TWENTY-NINE

Moments of clarity then black returned. Bits and pieces. The snow had gone, the river softened its grip on her. Back into the darkness. A wolf howled. A horse whinnied. She couldn't stay. A bright light engulfed her. Then blackness stole her away. A longing took hold of her for the embracing warmth of the light.

Something licked her face. In flashes of wonder, she viewed her life in quick succession as so many of her mother's patients had described at the brink of death. Tugging and more tugging.

"No, stop." She told them. "Leave me alone".

She wanted her mother, her Savior. Her body struggled for breath, but every attempt ended in a gurgling sound that lodged itself in her burning throat. Blackness took her again.

She swayed one way then another, then the water she had swallowed came up with a vengeance. Somehow, she found herself draped over Wind's back. She slipped again into unconsciousness.

She stirred and opened her eyes as hands pulled on her. She slid off Wind into someone's warm arms. She looked up through painful eyes and recognized the farmer's face smiling down at her. She searched the yard. Wind stood watching. Behind him in the distance, Little Sister sat at the edge of the tree line. Then, the dark took her again.

Shifting, shuffling, softness, warmth, then black again.

She heard voices. They seemed far away. She couldn't understand them.

".... Pneumonia.... Hypothermia.... Warm her slowly."

"Will she survive?" A woman's voice jarred Summer Sky awake.

They spoke English. She searched for the face of the farmer before slipping back into darkness.

"Mama." Summer Sky heard her voice rasp out of her agonized lungs. She couldn't breathe. Panic brought her awake. Night had come, and she had soft blankets over her. Her body screamed in pain. Her feet and hands throbbed. Her injured wrist had swelled as far as her skin's limits.

A scrape and a flicker of light joined her in the nightmare of pain. A woman lit a lamp on a table beside the bed.

She turned away from the light as it shot through the darkness and seared her swollen eyes. Every movement throbbed through her body and settled in her head.

"Drink this, honey. It will take the pain away."

Summer Sky obeyed. Waiting for the medicine's power, alleviating her pain. She struggled with every rattling, labored breath.

The woman who cared for her kept quiet. She pulled the blanket down and stripped off the heavy poultice across Summer Sky's bare chest.

The aromatic herbal scent wafted into her nose, and she smiled.

Garlic, mustard, and sage for sure. She added to the list pitch and needles of the fir or pine tree. She recognized her favorite aroma from the strong scent of the poultice, black cottonwood buds.

Comforted, she drifted back into a deep sleep.

She dreamt, but nothing made sense. Dark and light, cold and hot, fear and happiness all mingled into a giant nightmare. She grew exhausted sifting through the swing of her emotions. Tugging and ripping, snagging, and running, the dream may never end.

"Mama," Summer Sky cried out, but she couldn't find her.

She wept for her mother as arms encircled her. The person didn't smell like her mother.

"Fight, honey, fight, stay with us now." The stranger still rocked her, and she fell back into the dream.

Pain lashed at her, and she tried to run. Then she looked at her legs but couldn't find them. Fear sped up her heart until it hammered against her ribcage.

"You're nothing but a mutt!"

"If the fever breaks, she may recover."

"Your father loved you so."

Voices swam through her dream state, scraps of thought flit past as fast as the rushing water that had taken her down.

Stay, leave, fight, give in. Summer Sky couldn't decide through the wracking pain in her head. Light, dark, peace, fear. Confusion chased her across the expanse of shimmering, unreal space she ran through.

Lost, she turned in every direction, searching. For what? She couldn't identify. Her anxiety forced her on. She must find it, or she would die.

For a moment she wanted to wake up, but then the pain surfaced, and she forced herself back into the anxiety of her dream.

Wind stopped grazing and lifted his head, still chomping on grass that stuck out of his mouth. He looked at her for what seemed like a long time. Then he came and pulled her in with his big head and held her. She wrapped her arms around him and sighed. Nothing mattered but Wind.

He had stood steadfast beside her through everything. From the mean taunts of the children in the village. The deep grief from losing her mother and her home. His love steadfast beside her. She even grieved at losing the support and comfort of living in a community of people, despite the unfair treatment. She couldn't help that she had blue eyes. But Wind didn't care about the color.

The dream world dissipated along with her beloved horse as the pain increased. Cooking sounds broke through her groggy and scattered reasoning. The pain took her breath away, and she inhaled which brought on a spasm of coughing. She sat up in a soft bed, in a stranger's room. Someone patted her back hard until the mucous blocking her breath traveled into her mouth. A man's hand came from behind her with a cloth.

"Spit it out," he urged in a soft yet firm voice.

She obeyed as the sticky mass flew into the rag. With every spasm, the man folded the cloth and kept patting her back, dislodging more. Exhausted, Summer Sky slumped against the arm encircling her. Gentle hands laid her back onto a soft pillow and tidied the covers surrounding her.

She looked into the eyes of the farmer.

A woman came in and handed him a glass.

He cradled Summer Sky and placed the cup in her shaking hand, then helped her lift it. Drinking the warm liquid, she tasted honey and elderberry and lung wart. Her herbal medicine training assured her. She drank the whole thing, then laid back down, and watched the couple at her bedside. The woman had her arm around the shoulder of the farmer. Summer Sky should thank them for their kindness, but she couldn't find words in her feverish brain.

"Ah, you must wonder how you got here. Well, you rode in with your horse and a wolf that howls every night." He hesitated and looked at his wife. "My name is Charles, and this is my wife, Ida." He leaned closer and lifted her hand. His big hand dwarfed hers, warm and callused from the work on a farm, but comforting. He sniffed, and his wife patted him on the back.

"I…" Charles spoke, then coughed. He pulled his hanky from his shirt pocket and blew his nose with a loud honk.

Summer Sky looked from the farmer's face to his wife's. Charles and Ida. Should she recognize the names? These folks seem attached to her somehow. What does it mean?

Lord, I trust you know what you're doing.

"What we have wanted to say to you from the moment I saw you standing in the yard…" He hesitated.

His wife knelt and laid her hands on top of theirs. She wept openly at the side of the bed.

What's happening? The love in the room constricted her

congested chest and tears slipped down her face, dripping into her ears. Fear and longing warred in her heart. She couldn't understand why the love seemed directed at her.

Charles cleared his throat and swallowed so hard Summer Sky could hear his gulp. The Adam's apple in his neck moved up and down as he pulled her hand against his chest.

"What I'm trying to say is welcome home, Summer Sky." Charles' words carried to her on his sigh.

With a gasp, Summer Sky searched one face, then the other in confusion.

"How do you know my name?" Her words slipped past her constricted throat with a rasp.

God? Did you do this?

Summer Sky searched for her Lord's presence in the room and found it in the smiles and tear-streaked faces of Charles and Ida.

"Honey, it's a miracle. Your mother and father had chosen us as your Godparents when you were born. We stood beside them when you were christened. Even though we haven't seen you since your mother left, I would have known you anywhere, eyes as blue as the Summer Sky."

Ida rose to her feet and sat on the side of the bed. She opened her arms but seemed reluctant to hug her without permission. Perhaps, worried she might overwhelm her patient.

Summer Sky fell into her arms and wept. Ida rocked her and shushed her until the sobs subsided.

"You're home now, honey." Ida laid her against the pillow and tucked the quilt under her chin.

"You must rest now and get better. I'm sure you have a heap of questions. So do we, but we will have plenty of time for answers once you get better." Charles tucked Summer Sky's hand he still held under the covers and stepped away from the bed.

"Get some rest now, honey. I'll check in on you in a bit." Ida touched her face before she walked out of the room. Charles smiled at her as he closed the door with a quiet click.

She wondered if she still dreamt, or if she were in heaven.

She pinched herself and winced. No, not a dream and the pain seemed real enough.

Mama, can you believe it?

Lord, you did do this. You really did provide this farm for my salvation.

AFTERWORD

I spent last summer foraging and creating my own healing tinctures using Scott Cloos's book <u>Pacific Northwest Medicinal Plants</u> while I finished Her Name Is Summer Sky. All the references to natural medicinal plants ,Water Lily and Summer Sky had used, is from Scott's book.

I chose the Kalispel tribe because of a statement on their website <u>Kalispeltribe.com</u> regarding tolerance for white people and faith. Someone had stated the Kalispel's culture was "perhaps more cordial and hospitable than most Indian tribes". Because I respect indigenous cultures, I would never wish to insult a group of people. I did my best to keep that in mind as I researched and wrote this book, asking myself "could this have happened" staying as authentic as possible, despite being fiction.

The connection the Kalispels have to the land along the Pend Orielle River helped inspire this book. I too have grown up near the river. One summer, my mother took us to Manresa Grotto north of Newport, WA where local Kalispel people in the 1840's had church services. This was my first experience with our native neighbors and brought me a lifetime of respect and love for the culture.

Summer Sky's story came to me years ago in a dream, as most of my stories do. I couldn't get it out of my mind, so I developed it in my free time which took me two and a half years. I do become passionate about my characters as if they are part of my own family.

In Her Name Is Summer Sky, the fictional story begins with her differences becoming a target for bullying instead of celebration. In every culture there are bullies. I can contest that fact. Summer Sky, because she has blue eyes from her white father, is singled out in her mother's indigenous village by the other children.

Historically, atrocious things have happened to indigenous people that have suffered from the biggest bully of them all, government. The prohibition of whale hunting, the devastation of the buffalo population, the taking of the children and the robbing of land, the genocide for generations, all selfish acts against generous and gentle people. I pray God we have overcome this and still find a way to live together in peace. I do hope these atrocities can be forgiven by our native neighbors.

I work in an Elementary school. I see children of all nationalities being singled out for abuse by other students and know it isn't a racial issue but a societal heart condition. We do not choose what culture we are born to, but we can choose to love others, regardless of each other's differences.

That's why I wrote Summer Sky's story, and what she endured caused her to make choices she might not have, otherwise. I share her story as it is my own. There will always be people who want to shove others down to build themselves up. We must know the truth about ourselves since we are the only ones who truly know. The others who think they know, they don't. Don't listen.

How we treat others shows our heart condition and whether we choose good instead of evil.

In Her Name Is Summer Sky, I show one child who has been bullied. She has other challenges that cause greater strain on her than the bullies in her village.

I hope you like her story.

Keep an eye out for the sequel, Summer Sky: Savage Daughter.

I will set her in a different environment where I address the prejudices between white and native, and the failed social experiment of "kill the Indian and save the man" stated by Richard H. Pratt. In 1914 the residential school at Fort Spokane was permanently closed and the children were sent back to their families. But still, the attitude lived on in individual hearts to this day.

I set the second part of Summer Sky's story after 1918 and the Spanish flu that took so many lives. When Summer Sky grows through her teen years, she faces down the challenges of trying to fit into her father's world. Her bravery matches those who inspired this part of her story. The brave boys and girls who survived and told their stories so I could fill my pages with their voices.

Summer Sky's story may not end there, Summer Sky: Finding Home may turn out to be a love story! We shall see.

Thank you and may God bless you all for generations.

ABOUT THE AUTHOR

Le Anne Kemmish

I have been writing stories and journaling since I was in High School. I won't be saying how long ago that was. Writing has become a passion, an outlet, and a calling (sometimes in the middle of the night). Raised in the Pacific Northwest, I grew up camping, hiking, swimming, and loved the exhilarating feeling of climbing a tree all the way to the top until it swayed under my weight. As a middle child with five siblings, the outdoors was my great escape.

Learning to read took me longer than most, but once I caught on, I developed a lifelong love of the written word. Writing runs in the family, I credit my vivid word pictures to Great Uncle Ralph Waldo Emerson. My earliest composition was a secret admirer letter…to myself…when I was ten. I love writing adventurous "edge of your seat" suspense in wild places.

I still seek the outdoors. I enjoy all the seasons in my hometown. Winter skiing, snowshoeing, and curling up by the fire with a warm blanket; the interesting spring skies as the storms roll in; summer at the lake with hiking, swimming, kayaking, and boating; and fall with the crisp air, soft, warm sweaters and fuzzy socks to stay warm out at recess once school starts again.

I started working on Summer Sky's second book, Summer Sky: Savage Daughter. There will be a third book, Summer Sky: Finding Home.

My first two books, Zion Quest and Zion Lost, are about love, forgiveness, and a spiritual battle between good and evil.

I have other short stories and articles on my website Writing

Apples if you are interested in learning more about me.
I am honored to bring messages of hope and faith to my readers.

SUMMER SKY:

SAVAGE DAUGHTER
BOOK TWO OF THE SUMMER SKY SERIES

Le Anne Kemmish

CHAPTER ONE

With her checkered cotton apron in both hands, Ida brought a golden-crusted peach pie from the oven for after supper. She pushed open the window and sniffed the air as she set the pie on the windowsill to cool. The air smelled earthy, the first indication that spring would soon show itself.

She stood enjoying the fresh scene and heard gravel under a horse's hooves. Ida glanced across the road. The horse headed in their direction. Then she studied the childlike figure draped across the horse, as if... she couldn't say it.

"Charlie." Leaning out the window Ida screamed for her husband. She hurried as fast as her old legs could carry her. Her husband stepped from the barn door. He rushed in her direction, then turned toward where she headed. Charles reached the girl first.

Ida stopped short when she saw the wolf. It sat a distance away as if watching. She held her breath as Charles reached for Summer Sky.

"Is she..." Her voice trailed off.

"She's soaked through and as cold as ice. We must get her warm and dry, now. Run and get the Dr, quick." Ida ran ahead and left the door ajar for them. She put the warming bricks in the still hot oven and grabbed her coat. Charles brought Summer Sky into their grown daughter's old bedroom.

"Lord, don't let her die." Ida said a quick prayer as she rushed down the lane. The Doctor kept an office on the main street of their tiny town.

"Dr. Jenson, we need you." Ida rasped, out of breath, as soon as she stepped into the small waiting room. The doctor sat reading a newspaper in his chair by the fire.

"Something happen to Charles?" He stood, set his folded newspaper on the side table, then stepped toward the counter and grabbed his medical bag.

"No, it's a girl that showed up half-frozen." She held the door as the Dr slipped into his coat and grabbed his hat off a peg beside the door.

* * *

Waiting for the doctor, Charles worked at removing the wet clothing from Summer Sky's cold body. Her bare feet, blue with cold, had him worried. He tugged on the elk fur wrapped around her, but it wouldn't give way. He discovered the rope twined around the girl's torso but couldn't find the knot. Time ticked past. He took out the knife he carried in his pocket and sliced through the rope, freeing the child of the sodden skin. Next, he pulled the parka over her head, and she yelped in pain.

Summer Sky cradled her left arm even in her unconscious state. Charles looked closer, noticing the swelling. She had secured the arm against her chest. He wondered if she had more injuries. He wouldn't move her anymore until the Dr examined her.

"Heat. She needs heat." Charles rushed into the kitchen for their foot warming bricks. Searching for them, it dawned on him that his efficient wife must have set them in the oven before she left.

He pulled the flannel cases out of the drawer and dropped the bricks into them. He placed them on both sides of her body under the warm blankets and prayed for healing.

"Where's that Dr.?" Charles pacing the room, helpless. The door flew open, and Ida rushed into the room.

"Did you get her wet clothes off?" Ida asked. He noticed a bloom of heat crawl up his face. She gave him an understanding nod. "Please, go grab one of my night dresses for her. I will strip the wet clothes off her myself."

Happy to leave her to that task, he left the room. Dr. Jenson passed him with an encouraging smile and closed the door behind him.

* * *

Charles brought two chairs into the room and set them beside the bed. The child moaned and jerked in her unconsciousness. The pitiful thing must be in pain. Dr. Jenson came back into the room stirring a white substance in a glass of water.

"Help me sit her up, Charles. Let's see if we can get her to take this." Charles leaned over and scooped Summer Sky into his arms with as much gentleness as he could muster and sat behind her.

"She's skin and bones." Charles commented as her shoulder blade pressed against his ribs.

"Yes, she must have gone through a lot it seems. We must focus on getting her well." The Dr held the cup to her lips and waited for a response.

"Come on, honey, drink up. You need it for the pain." Charles coaxed, and Summer Sky opened her mouth and swallowed with a sour grimace across her pallid face.

Ida came in with more bricks wrapped in flannel.

"Warm her slowly or she may go into shock. I've set her broken wrist which should alleviate some of the pain there. She has cuts and bruising on her legs and a couple of lumps on her head. Give her the poppy opiate powder every three hours but not sooner. If she cries out, you may dose her with feverfew and ghost pipe tincture. Mindful of the dosage. My guess she weighs less than half of your weight, Ida. No offense."

"None taken, Dr. She looks near starved with her ribs showing like that."

"Give her half doses between the poppy opiate powder. "

"I will."

"I'll check back in on her in the morning."

"Thank you, Carl," Charles said as he escorted the Dr to the door.

When he returned, his heart constricted seeing Ida leaning against the bed on her knees. Her lips moved in prayer. He joined her intercession for the Goddaughter he hadn't seen in ten years, minus the brief encounter where she had stolen food from them.

He reached for Ida's hand and bowed his head.

"Lord, thank you for bringing Summer Sky home. We pray she recovers. Your will is what we ask. We pray her recovery is your will, is all. Thanks again, in Jesus' name, Amen."

"Amen." Ida repeated as she reached up and swiped a strand of hair off the girl's face, tucking it behind her ear. She sat in one of the chairs. Charles joined her.

"Oh, Charles, I hate to say this but I'm afraid Water Lily

must have died from the Spanish flu epidemic. She would never have left Summer Sky to fend for herself."

"I thought the same thing when she came for food. What I don't understand is how she showed up here of all places. Maybe Water Lily told her about us and where we lived if they had problems." Charles thought for a moment.

"Perhaps God himself guided the horse to us. And, the wolf, I don't think he has taken his eyes off the house for one minute."

"It gives me shivers just thinking about that thing watching us," Ida mused.

"It's waiting for Summer Sky, I'm thinking. The horse doesn't seem to mind it, so I'm not too worried. As long as it stays away from our chickens.